THE DWARF LAUGHED, HIS TWISTED LITTLE BODY SHAKING WITH GLEE . . .

He liked to see a beautiful woman tortured.

THE GIANT WITH THE MIND OF A CHILD STARED UNBLINKINGLY . . .

He didn't understand the terrible scene before him.

THE GIRL WAS BORED, HER BEAUTIFUL FACE BETRAYING NO EMOTION . . .

She had seen the scars, heard the screams too often.

THE COUNT SEETHED WITH RAGE, VENOM TWISTING HIS FEATURES . . .

He was going to prolong the agony for a long time.

They were in the vast meeting hall of the Teutonic Knights. Before them, on a large table, lay a woman—blonde, lovely, her eyes enormous with fear. From her head and heart, wires ran to a small control panel next to the Count.

"In three seconds, I can turn her into a blank-eyed moron who cringes or fawns at the lift of an eyebrow," the Count screamed. Then he addressed the big American by his side.

"IT IS YOUR TURN NEXT, NICK CARTER!"

THE NICK CARTER/KILLMASTER SERIES

NICK CARTER

A Killmaster Spy Chiller

THE BRIGHT BLUE DEATH

AWARD BOOKS
NEW YORK

TANDEM BOOKS
LONDON

Second Award printing 1968

Dedicated to

The Men of the Secret Services

of the

United States of America

AWARD BOOKS are published by:
Universal Publishing & Distributing Corporation
235 East Forty-fifth Street, New York, N. Y. 10017

TANDEM BOOKS are published by:
Universal-Tandem Publishing Co. Ltd.,
33 Beauchamp Place, London, SW3, England

Manufactured in the United States of America

CHAPTER 1

TO THE NORTH the sky flickered weirdly like a menacing storm that threatened to come down with all its fury. This flickering was like no other storm; it seemed magnified many, many times over. It was as if the cosmos had ignited of its own gases and was blowing itself out on this remote shore of the universe. As the great sheets of neon-colored flames licked the night sky in terrible silence, they struck some atavistic chord in the minds of the men in the boat, making them uneasy and stirring buried recollections of a forgotten era. These were the northern lights in an unusually colorful display for this late in the season.

The chord it struck in the mind of the big American who stood on the plunging bow of the sloop was pure anger. Twenty minutes ago the aurora had been blotted from sight by a blanket of fog and things had been as they should. Weather reports, the best money could buy from analysis of the Tiros satellite photographs and a special U2 flight from an American base in Spain, had guaranteed thick fog on this date blanketing Northern Europe and the Southern Scandinavian countries all night long. On the strength of those reports the ancient wooden sloop had beat down the choppy, tide-wracked waters of the Kattegat for two days and nights and was finishing its clandestine trip toward its destination off the Swedish coast. The fog had been so thick you could heat and serve it to the crew. But now to the south the stars were clearly visible and in the northern sky so were the lights. Even the Swedish coast was visible, a darker line against the sky and water. Well, so much for technology in weather prediction.

Now he stood with one hand lightly on a stay, balancing easily against the chop while he calculated the effects of this latest development as coldly as a riverboat gambler watching the dealer bust his flush. Finally he decided not to abort the mission. And at that moment above the sound of the waves and the keening wind in the rigging, he heard the harsh voice of the old man at the wheel.

"I tank we coom far enough now, Mister," he said.

The American looked toward his companion, a younger man standing in the shadows, and shook his head negatively.

"Espionage," the big American said, "is just one God damned thing after another." Then he went back to the captain.

"Another five miles, Lars," he said, "that was the deal. It's a long cold swim and our air won't hold out forever."

The old captain shook his head.

"Fog is blown off, yar? No goot to come closer for me. Inside dis forbitten zone they shoot first. Yar, then talk afterwards—maybe."

The American could only see the lower half of the old man's face. Lit by the light of the binnacle compass it was seamed and grizzled by years of hardship. And at the moment it was set with the stubbornness of a man who has found a truth. The American stared at him a moment and then shrugged.

"All right, Lars, hold her steady as she goes. We'll need a few minutes to get into the gear."

"Yar," the Swede said noncommittly. The big American beckoned to his younger companion and they both went below. Together they checked the gear laid out neatly in the cabin. It had, of course, been checked out half a dozen times before but the big American went over it again as carefully as if he had bought it at dockside from a particularly untrustworthy merchant. Eventually he appeared satisfied. The young crew-cut American watched the actions of the bigger one carefully, almost with awe.

The dim light of the single cabin lamp illuminated the older man's features with the harsh contrasts of an old woodcut. It showed a face that might have belonged to a Renaissance princeling. In the shadows the stronger features flourished. Courage, strength, resolution and intelligence dominated. A suggestion of humor about the eyes, a sensual mouth and a grace and quickness were also there. The face belonged to a man named Nick Carter, better known to the secret services of the world as N3, Killmaster.

"One thing, N3," the young American said. "We're still outside the sub nets at the channel mouth."

The older man nodded as if the problem were trifling. He wasn't really much older than his crew-cut companion but his face made the difference. The face seemed about a thousand years older and had a strength of character that the younger one might never acquire.

"We'll go under them, Chet," he said finally. "You've made a lot deeper dives than that. We don't have much choice. Old Lars is getting scared and I don't much blame him. Without the fog to cover him he's a sitting duck." The young man nodded.

For some time afterwards there was silence as they donned the complex diving gear. Then they mounted the companionway, balancing between steps against the sway and surge of the old sloop. Outside the night was clear but rough, with the wind blowing the tops of waves into a driving spray. As soon as they emerged on deck the old Swedish skipper brought the sloop up into the wind as a sign that he wasn't going another cable length further into the forbidden zone. The boat lost way, bobbing and rolling in the heavy chop, the sails cracking like rifle fire.

"Good luck, lads," Lars said. He watched them make their final preparations without much curiosity.

"Same to you, old-timer," the big man said. "Don't spend all those dollars on one woman."

"Har, har," the Swede laughed. "I tank I too old for dat now."

"Never too old," the American said cheerfully. "I wouldn't put it past you an inch. And another thing. Don't try to sell those anti-radar boxes for another couple of months or you'll end up in jail for sure."

The younger American shuffled impatiently. All this fooling around when there was a mission under way. Nick Carter concealed a smile. He'll learn, Nick thought.

"I bane in jail before," the Swede laughed. "I tank I rather go to jail than go with you. Dey put you on top of atomic bomb and shoot you off to da moon, I'm tinking, har, har."

He laughed as if he'd made a great joke. He was still laughing when the Americans hit the water. A few seconds later the sail of the sloop filled and the old man's laughter was drowned by the hissing of the wind and the Americans were alone in the water.

It took them a minute or two to adjust themselves to the big battery-driven sea scooters that would pull them through the water much faster than they could swim. The young American watched the sky and spoke in a queer flat voice.

"Geez, they oughta label this 'Operation Science Fiction' instead of 'Operation Bernadotte' or whatever it is. First this weird mission and then take a look at those lights," he said, pointing at the sky. "It's kinda like a preview of the last day or something."

Nick answered with a short, kindly obscenity. He understood the younger man's reaction to the strangeness of the night and the mission but it would be a great deal better for both of them if they kept their minds strictly on the details of the work ahead without complicating it with psychological factors. Nick gave the go sign and without any further words the two men dived and set out on the last leg of their long trip toward the forbidden island.

Musko, Sweden, an island of granite, was one of thousands of such granite skerries, islands and peninsulas along Sweden's rugged south coast. On the island was a city. And the city had everything other cities had and a bit more—garages, theatres, hotels, offices, manufacturing plants, etc., and even an air base with army and navy installations. The only difference was that everything was underground, buried beneath the granite of the island, safe from anything but a direct hit with a hydrogen warhead and perhaps even from that.

While other nations spent their millions searching for the biggest bombs for their bucks or rumbles for their rubles, the men who guided Sweden's affairs had set newly developed, high-speed drills to work after World War II and had turned the rock wilderness of their south coast into a haven where a whole population might find refuge from the terrible realities of the nuclear age. It was estimated that in the event of holocaust and if the new experiment worked, as many as ninety per cent of Sweden's people would find refuge in the vast underground cities, of which this was the first, and that after waiting months until the air was again clean, Sweden would emerge with its people, prosperity and technology still intact.

Of course other nations had "hardened" command posts and missile sites, but nothing for civilians. Only the Swedes had solved the vast psychological problems, the ventilation problems, the storage problems and a million others to make the network of under-rock cities a reality.

And then, suddenly, betrayal. A high-ranking Swedish officer, one Colonel Wennerstrom, had defected to the Russians with vital information concerning Musko and its defenses. The relocation of the defenses had cost millions. And for the first time, the Swedes were uneasy with their underground refuge; they realized that it had an Achilles heel.

Since then sophisticated jet fighter planes on constant alert could be scrambled from the bowels of the earth in a matter of seconds to investigate or blast an intruder. A dozen different radar systems scanned the surrounding sea and sky, and the pine-clad slopes could open like something out of science fiction to release destroyers that lurked in underground harbors, cleared for action against any vessel that ventured inside the well-marked "Forbidden Zones."

Since the Wennerstrom affair, the Swedes were playing for keeps.

Nick Carter was well aware of all this as he moved smoothly through the black water off Musko. It was impossible for anyone to get inside the zone by accident. If they did—well, the results might be regrettable but what was one life compared with the future of a nation, perhaps of mankind. So reasoned the Swedes.

Nevertheless, Nick had laid his bet as follows: He would undertake to infiltrate the subterranean island fortress despite the best efforts of Swedish security and military forces to stop him. All Nick asked was a free hand to operate, certain equipment and another agent of his own choosing.

To Hawk, the lean, tough old man who was head of AXE, the United States' highest and most secret intelligence agency, Nick had remarked, "Man has built nothing that another good man can't get into or out of if he wants to badly enough. At least that's my experience." And his experience was considerable.

Hawk had looked thoughtfully at his top agent, the man they called Killmaster, and chomped down hard on the end of the dead cigar that hung from his thin lips, saying, "Change it to a good man *stands a chance* of getting in or out and I'll buy it. Still," he added dryly, "I'd hate to lose a man of your ability and experience just trying to prove a point. The Explorers Club is down the street if it's adventure you seek. If the Swedes have security problems, why not let them solve them themselves?"

"How about NORAD?" Nick asked softly.

"Mmmmm," said Hawk and shifted the cigar from one side of his mouth to the other. "How about NORAD is right." He thought it over. Both men were aware that the

North American Air Defense headquarters, the nerve center of America's air defense umbrella, was cut into a mountain in Colorado similar to the Musko setup. If Musko could be infiltrated, the same technique could be used to infiltrate and eventually neutralize NORAD, leaving America utterly defenseless from attack by air. The thought was chilling.

"Give me a list of what you'll need and pick the agent you want to go with you," Hawk had said finally.

Nick had picked Chet, a seasoned agent with an engineering degree and expertise in speleology and underground navigation. Separately they had arrived in a small Swedish fishing village and set up headquarters. Then Nick had set out to learn everything there was to know about the military civil defense establishment at Musko. Both were expert intelligence men. As they worked and talked and studied, a picture of the Musko base began to take shape.

Among the other things they learned was that their mission wasn't as theoretical as it had appeared when first proposed by the Swedish military attaché in Washington. There were rumors. . . . As professionals the AXEmen put little stock in unconfirmed rumors but at embassy cocktail parties and informal gatherings of newsmen one was given to understand that top Swedish security was worried that a certain nameless Asian country, bordered by Russia and the China Sea, had a deep and active interest in Musko and its sister cities under rock. Some officials even suspected that infiltration was going on right now. . . .

Far below the tormented surface of the Baltic, the sea scooter drew the two AXEmen steadily toward Musko. From time to time as he swam, Nick flashed the beam of a powerful electric torch ahead of him. There was a chance that a patrolling aircraft might spot the light but it was one that he had to take. Presently the submarine net appeared in the beam like a strange undersea spider-web.

Nick signaled the other AXEman. Of course he could cut the net, that would be the quickest way, but when the strands parted they would activate a light on a control board ashore that would reveal their positions exactly. Much the same would happen if they swam over the tops of the nets—they would break a photo-electric beam. Killmaster had thoroughly researched modern basic security setups. Nick knew the only way into the city unobserved was through the net.

The two AXE agents surfaced briefly to talk things over.

"How are you doing, Chet?" Nick asked.

"It ain't Bahamas waters but then we've done ten times harder than this in the old Purge tank."

He was referring to the so-called torture survival school that each AXE agent endured periodically in order to ready himself for the rigors of upcoming missions.

"Okay," Nick nodded approval. "This will be deep and tiring but as you say we've done lots tougher." He checked the radium dial of his watch. "There's no need to hurry but let's not waste any time either. Take it easy and steady and in twenty minutes we'll be knocking at the Swedes' back door."

The younger man grinned in the darkness and then they started down, using the web of the sub nets to guide them. The water became steadily colder as they descended through the inky blackness, fathom after fathom. Nick kept an eye on his depth indicator. Just over two hundred feet down the edge of the net was waiting . . . deeper, deeper . . . what was that?

A golden stiletto, its blade bright and the handle embossed with the finest of ancient workmanship. It didn't say "For the bravest" or have his initials on it but Nick knew it was for him. Then a hand reached out to take the dagger. Nick recognized the face behind it. Others reached out and these faces too were familiar.

Popes and kings and generals from the bloody pages of history strove for the enchanted stiletto but a great presence forbid them; the dagger was for Nick Carter, Killmaster. Nick seized the weapon and was delighted with its perfect balance and fine workmanship. A fierce joy enveloped him, an electric excitement ran through him. Suddenly, an aurora dazzled his eyes, a great flashing jewel in the murky depths. Out of it appeared women, all the women of the world, whose bodies undulated just beyond his reach and they cried out to him with murmurs of passion—all the women he had ever known from sultry nights at the edge of hot Caribbean breakers to cool evenings with lovely white bodies that served his pleasure with sobs of joy in European cities. Nick was wild with happiness. Everything in the world seemed to come roaring together to center in him. He wanted more than anything else to swim immediately to the surface with the magic stiletto and make off with the secret of its power.

A man nearby laughed sardonically. The man pointed out that to do so would mean a lingering and sublimely agonizing death from the bends or drowning—odds of six to five, you pick 'em. Nick was mildly surprised to see that the laughing man was himself. His own mind, cold and detached, was telling him that he was showing exaggerated symptoms of nitrogen narcosis, *les ivresses des grandes profondeurs* as the French called it. It had happened to him on every deep dive he had ever made and would on every one he ever would make. The deep dive affected the composition of his blood and the blood affected his brain. The second man told him the *rapture of the depths* would pass shortly and he would once again be a hardnosed AXE operative instead of some strange submarine mystic. Even now the giddiness and delusions were wearing off, and although Nick had experienced the symptoms many times, he had never felt them as strongly as this before. With a rueful grin at the glimpse of his subconscious that the nitrogen narcosis had produced,

Nick turned to check out the other AXEman's reaction to the depths. What he saw jolted him into action. Nick saw the pale, exultant face of a madman. Death was written on the young AXEman's gaping face.

Chet was still deep within the grips of the nitrogen narcosis. His mask was off and a trail of bubbles led from his mouth toward the surface. His sea scooter cut elaborate arabesques through the blackness, weaving up and down and around. As the light from Nick's beam fell on him a sly, taunting look came into Chet's eyes. Before Nick could catch him and jam the air tubes back into his mouth he dodged and shot out of range, tearing out of Nick's clutching grasp to stop a short distance away.

Nick tried again, tried desperately, edging up closer, hoping the momentarily deranged AXEman would hold still for a few seconds longer so Nick might save his life. But some drunken impulse in the other man's mind jolted him to his doom—the sea scooter turned and sped away into the darkness. The sleds were identical models, evenly matched for speed. The man was surely dead by now. Nick could only watch the sea scooter with its macabre burden as it bore steadily away into the black vault of the Baltic.

A shiver that had little to do with the cold of the water chilled the spine of the surviving American. It was a well-known phenomenon that divers under the grip of the delirium of the depths had an urge to take off their masks. It usually passed and was always controllable. Almost always, Nick amended grimly. Chet's remark just after going into the water had indicated his state of mind. Perhaps he should have foreseen . . .

Nick rejected the thought with finality. There was no point in second guessing himself. Nick was part of an infiltration team—not a wet nurse. And AXEmen learned early in their careers to leave their dead where they fell. He looked at his watch. For the second time tonight he must decide whether or not to abort the mission. And he must make up his mind pretty damn fast. Soon all hell was going to break loose in this channel. Killmaster had seen to that.

CHAPTER 2

IN THE DETRITUS of the sea bottom where the island sloped into the Baltic Nick crouched, a hulking alien form, while around him in the blackness a thousand invisible eyes watched the intruder. The needle on his reserve air tank fell steadily lower but there was nothing he could do but sit in the ooze of this northern clime and wait. . . .

Then a chilly light suffused the darkness of the ocean floor. Nick smiled behind his face plate. The timing was perfect. It was time to go. He swam toward the light.

The water around him stirred violently. High above his head, on the surface, a long black shadow ghosted by, churning the water to cream. A patrol destroyer on crash alert. It was all part of his plan. The electronic "joke box" he had left bobbing around on the sound was timed to start sending signals at exactly this minute. They would show up on the Swedish radar screens as an intruder the size of a heavy cruiser. The image would dance tauntingly around the screen for a few hours and then disappear. It was the only way he had been able to think of that would guarantee opening the great hydraulically operated nets of the cave-harbor opening at the exact moment when Nick Carter was outside wanting in.

It was a good plan and working to perfection. He made it through the entrance just as he saw the great hydraulic booms beginning to slide the net shut behind him. They certainly weren't wasting any time. He hoped the old Swede Lars had made it well up the coast by now. With this kind of "bogey" on their screens, the Swedish destroyer commanders would have itchy trigger fingers tonight.

Presently the pilings of the destroyer dock appeared

before his face plate. Nick swam well under the dock and then surfaced for his first view of the underground island.

At first glance it resembled a small naval installation anywhere. A few small patrol boats were tied up at the docks, loading cranes towered over the bigger slips, railroad tracks led off from loading sheds into the darkness and blue dungareed swabbies could be seen moving purposefully about or grabbing a fast smoke on the fantail. But then he noticed the great vaulting arch of the cathedral-like cavern. Seeing the cavern was as startling as waking up in the twenty-first century.

Nick shook his head. It had been a strange mission from the beginning, out of his regular line. He was glad that it was almost over. Before he could begin the landing stage of his infiltration, heavy footsteps pounded over his head. Then came a gruff voice full of obscenities that he hadn't had time to learn during his crash course in Swedish at Georgetown University. He could make out the gist of it though, and he relaxed. The voice had nothing to do with him.

"I don't care if it is the end of the world, swabbie, the Swedish Navy doesn't leave lines trailing in the water. Aboard one of the old schooners I'd have had the skin off your back."

A sulky, juvenile voice answered, "Aye, aye," and the footsteps receded. Nick grinned. Mankind might reach the stars or be forced underground but warrant officers never changed.

When he was sure that the dock above him was empty, he sat himself on a supporting timber and stripped off his rubber suit, weighted it and watched it sink to the bottom. Then he slipped into the fatigue shirt and dungarees of the Swedish Navy. The uniform fitted loosely enough to conceal about his person a great deal of specialized equipment which he took from a waterproof belly pack.

He took extra care with his weapons, his three darlings:

Wilhelmina, the custom made stripped-down 7mm Luger, Hugo, the exquisitely balanced stiletto and Pierre, the minuscule sphere of deadly nerve gas that he wore strapped between his legs.

Silently he eased himself out from under the dock, grasped the rungs of the ladder and climbed to dock level. With one feline surge of his powerful shoulders he pulled himself upright on the dock and walked swiftly away. As he walked Nick looked around for a broom to carry. Nobody bothers a man with a broom—that was true in all armies since the Caesars. No luck.

Suddenly an officer appeared out of nowhere. "Hey, swabbie," he snapped. "That means you, sailor."

Nick stopped. It felt as though every eye in the place was on him.

"Tuck in your shirt tail and stop loitering."

Nick let a vacant grin spread across his features as he saluted and tucked in the offending shirt tail. Then he walked with renewed speed down the dock toward the great granite wall. No one paid any attention to him. He passed a warehouse office where a petty officer was drinking coffee and reading a magazine. He stepped across a set of railroad tracks and walked to the wall of the cave as if he knew just what he was doing. Which he did. He found, as he had known he would, a metal stairway that led to a catwalk used for repairing the wiring. Nick proceeded along it until he came to a steel ladder anchored to the rock face of the cavern and rising to the arc lights mounted in the ceilings. Nick began to ascend the ladder.

At the top of the ladder he stopped. Far below the great hydraulic doors of the cave slid open and he saw the destroyer backing into its dock. The sailors looked like toys and the destroyer like a plastic ship model.

Above his head the giant air-conditioning duct yawned. With the other vents it was part of a network that ran through the underground city. With destroyer class ships and the trains and tractors needed to service them the underground installations would become death traps without gigantic air-conditioning systems. With the exception of the sub net incident the carefully laid plan had worked like a dream. Now N3 saw a major difficulty staring him in the face.

The trouble was the vent was just a bit high. He had been prepared to handle that but it was to have been a two man operation. If he stood on the rail of the catwalk he might just be able to jump and catch the rim of the air-conditioning unit. He looked thoughtfully at the harbor below him. Hitting the water from this height would make an awful mess out of a man.

Carefully he worked the hand grips tight on his two best assets: a pair of sub-miniaturized electromagnets that tested out at five hundred pounds. The magnets were to take him up and down the sheet iron ventilating shafts like a human fly—click on, click off—a lovely gadget as long as you didn't break the rhythm and click both off at the same time.

Then doing his best not to look down at what could be a nightmarish free fall to where the tiny sailors walked about on concrete, Nick raised himself to the round metal rail, balancing against the wall with his fingertips. His hands were sweating slightly now and his pulse rate was way up. He forced himself to look straight at the wall until he became calm. The slightest shift in his weight could send him skidding off the rail and then down two hundred feet to the concrete and water below.

The opening of the air-conditioning vent was a scant foot above his fingers. Normally his powerful legs could easily flick him many times that distance into the air from a standing position. But not on this tractionless tubing. One misstep and he'd go down, not up.

A cold voice within him said: *Pack it in, Carter. This was a two-man job from the beginning.* He could feel the sweat break out again. He took a deep breath and looked a second time. The air-conditioning vent was where it had been, not an inch closer.

"No," he said audibly to his inner voice. Then he jumped.

For a moment he was out in space, his hands clawing at air and terror constricting every nerve and organism in his great body. Then his hands were grabbed by the force of the magnets which slammed them against the metal of the duct and locked him up against the cold stone of the cavern's ceiling.

With a lithe effort he wriggled over the lip of the vent, switched off the magnets and sat on the edge. That, thought Nick, deserves a cigarette. The air conditioning would twist and turn throughout the city and while Nick knew the route in a general way, Chet, the spelunker, the expert in crawling around the blackness of caves, would have gotten them to their destination a lot faster.

The dinner party was over and her guests had departed. All but one. Astrid Lundgren sat on the porch of her ultra-modern home on the coast of Musko, fingering her sterling silver liqueur glass and wishing that he, too, would take himself off. It didn't seem likely that he would. The young man was well-socked into the chaise longue across from her and carrying on about the wonders of the northern lights as if this were the first time the aurora had been seen in Sweden.

"We'll try the next series at twenty thousand oscillations per minute allowing, naturally, for a kinetic fall-off factor of X over Y in the generator bindings," Astrid said.

"What's that?" the young man asked.

"I'm sorry," Astrid said, "I was thinking out loud."

"Astrid," the young man said, "you are impossible. You are not a woman but a machine. Do you know what you are called among the officials of Musko? You are called—"

"I am not concerned with the marginal bestiality of

otherwise competent officials," the woman cut in. She looked at her guest with lazy boredom. He was tall and blond and handsome as an Adonis. In addition he had represented Sweden on the Olympic ski team and was now making his way rapidly up the ladder of the Swedish Security establishment. For some strange reason Vice Admiral Larson, head of Security, liked him. As far as Astrid was concerned she was sorry she had ever encouraged the young athlete, but her friends had been urging her to have more of a social life.

"They call you the Swedish Iceberg," the young man said. They called her a great many other things, as Astrid was well aware, but she couldn't afford to let that bother her. Time was short for Sweden and men were fools to be irritated when a handsome woman chose to devote her life to duty rather than the dubious pleasure of playing handmaiden to a husband. Knute was irritated and jealous, for Astrid's devotion to duty had not been unsuccessful. She was head of Engineering Planning for the complete series of underground refuges and military bases.

So all the answer she needed to make to the young man was an indolent shrug.

"Some day you will overstep yourself, Knute."

She reclined in the chair, her long full legs stretched haphazardly, her skirt showing enticing stretches of magnificent thigh. Her head was back, accenting the promise of the wide mouth with the bee-stung lips, the high cheekbones and the green eyes that went so well with flowing hair so blond it was as white as hoar frost. But even in casual Sweden few men had tasted that promise.

Knute came and sat his athlete's body on the chaise longue beside her and ran his hand along the fine strong bones of her cheeks, down her white neck to where her magnificent breasts were barely confined by the bodice of her cocktail dress. His voice became caressing and wandered as low as his hands.

"Cara mia," he whispered, "ice goddess, you are driving me mad. My nights have been a torment."

Astrid sat completely still under his insistent assault, neither resisting nor encouraging.

"Yes, Astrid, you are well named, you are like a star so cold and distant in your perfection . . ."

Does he think I'm a child to believe such chatter? Astrid thought.

" . . . but a strange star. Perhaps men are not to your liking. Perhaps the softness of women is preferable."

"If you mean, will I sleep with you to prove that I am not a Lesbian, the answer is no," Astrid said in her infuriatingly well-controlled voice.

"Ah, but you will," Knute said. His voice was strangely hoarse. Astrid wished she hadn't served him those last two drinks.

"I will fan that banked fire within you to a holocaust, my darling," Knute groaned. His face was up against her neck showering it with ardent kisses; one strong hand cupped the amplitude of her left breast and the other hand reached beneath her skirt. Astrid attempted to struggle free but Knute was too strong.

For a moment she considered giving in. After all, perhaps she had led him on. Then she thought: *If I give in now, his conceit will be boundless and I will never be free of him.*

She twisted free of his grasp, feeling the top of her gown rip away from her body.

"Knute," she gasped. "I am due shortly at the laboratory. . . ."

"The lab," he snorted, "your bloody precious lab. Not tonight, sweetheart."

She knew that standing there, her breasts bare, was like waving a red flag at a bull. She darted for the door but he cut her off, pinned her against it and succeeded in tearing away the rest of her dress. His powerful body was forcing her toward the floor when she managed once again to break free. She ran blindly toward the trees at the back of the house, not knowing whether she was laughing or crying.

Knute's footsteps thudded close behind her. Then he caught her by one wrist, his grip as strong as a vise. Astrid acted instinctively. She lashed out with the side of one bare foot and knocked his legs from under him while her free hand drove a karate chop at his chin. As the blond giant started to fall, she caught his wrist and twisted his body around in the air. He landed hard, his face driven into the carpet of pine needles beneath the trees. Astrid held onto his arms and placed a bare foot firmly in the middle of his back.

"Behave," she said.

"Bitch," he grunted.

"Will you be nice if I let you up?" she asked.

"I'll finish you," he ground out.

"Knute," she said trying a different tack, "you are a fine specimen of Swedish manhood, handsome and virile. But our country is approaching a crisis, as you well know. If our physicists do not find a way to prevent it, the Chinese will shortly have a laser beam that can cut through the granite of Musko like a knife through hot butter. Then we shall all be back where we started. You see, therefore, why I have no interest in anything these days but finding that defense. Perhaps later when the crisis is past."

As she spoke Knute's ardor cooled. Being bested in hand to hand combat by a beautiful woman and being forced to eat pine needles cools the most inflamed libido. Presently she let him up. With a brief and very formal apology Knute took his leave and stalked in injured dignity to his car.

Disturbed and a little absent-minded, Astrid wandered back to her house, found some clothes which she tossed on helter-skelter, then went out and got into the little British sports car which was her only vice.

The angry whine of the sports car shattered the solemn silence of the dark woods as she sped back to the under-

ground lab. True, she would be a little early for the first
shift but there was much on her mind and the lab was
peaceful. There she was usually able to order her thoughts
before drifting into concentration on the problems of
countering the Chinese laser. As she drove toward the
refuge of the lab, her thoughts were confused. Knute was
a nice boy. Like hell, he was a lunkhead. . . . The Chinese
were close to completing their laser. She was reassured by
the fact that the Chinese would never really develop the
weapon that could pierce the granite of Musko without
actually infiltrating a team of technologists to run surveys
on the island. . . . At least Vice Admiral Larson and his
fair-haired boys like Knute were preventing that from
happening. She felt sure there wasn't a mackerel in the
water or a sea gull in the air that Larson's men didn't
know about.

"Hello, sweetheart, let's see your pass."

The grandfatherly guard under the fluorescent light at
the entrance to the laboratory building had known her
since she was a skinny kid hanging around her daddy's lab
but he still wanted her pass. That was security.

She parked the sports car and ascended in the elevator
by herself to her lab. As the familiar corridors closed
around her, her mind went automatically toward her job.
Astrid thought she had a pretty good idea of the development of the Chicom laser. And she thought she had the
answer. It was kind of a force field that would dissipate
the effect of any laser, based on the well-known fact that
mass bends light rays. The trouble was that people working on the force field project kept dying.

There was apparently some kind of emission from the
force field that killed lab workers like the X rays did at
the turn of the century. Scientific congresses were demanding that experiments be halted until the msyterious emission was isolated and tamed. But there was so little time.
. . .

The lab was deserted, as it always was between early
and late shifts, but her Assistant Chief of Projects would

be on hand. Astrid drew two cups of coffee from an urn and walked toward the door of his office.

At the office door she dropped both cups of coffee, scalding her ankles, and jammed her wrist in her mouth to keep from screaming.

Knudson, her Assistant Chief of Project lay slumped on the floor. Astrid wanted to scream until her lungs ached.

Knudson's skin was blue. Not the slight purplish tinge of suffocation or a coronary seizure but a vivid startling blue—blue like a china plate, dark and shiny. His white hair stood out against the shiny blue of the bald spot on his scalp. Astrid was seized with an hysterical desire to laugh. Lying there dead on the carpet, Knudson reminded her of a piece of Dutch Delftware.

She grabbed the door frame to keep from falling and took a deep breath. The mysterious indigo rays, as the technical journals had called them, had struck again. No one had been able to discover their cause but their effect was obvious.

Astrid wondered if it were safe to approach the body. What was the life of the rays? Slowly her famous self-possession took over. Her watch told her that the early shift would be arriving soon. If one of them caught a look at Knudson there wouldn't be a laboratory worker in Sweden who would work with the force field. She couldn't help thinking what a boon that would be to the Chicoms.

The procedure of course was to get hold of Vice Admiral Larson and let him handle the matter. But workers would be arriving any minute.

Quickly Astrid foraged around the laboratory. Then clad in a lead-lined smock and hood she approached the body. The dead weight was difficult but finally she managed to move the body a foot and once she had it going it became easier. After a macabre tussle in which she got the hysterical impression that the dead man wanted to dance with her, she succeeded in bringing Knudson upright and forcing him into her private closet.

Ten minutes later the irreproachable Astrid Lundgren greeted the first early reporting lab worker with her customary distant politeness and assigned him a routine job.

CHAPTER 3

NICK HAD BEEN moving along the system of gigantic air-conditioning ducts for well over an hour now. An infrared flashlight and infrared sensitive glasses made the tunnel clear as day. Not that there was much to see. The corridors unwound themselves with monotonous regularity. All Nick had to do was be sure that he didn't get himself sucked in to an air-pusher fan or an air-purifying chemical bath.

Nick intended to find his way to the nuclear reactor that powered most of the island, take a few pictures and report to the office of the Security Director to show that he'd gone thoroughly unauthorized and undetected from the outside world into the heart of the top secret areas of the Musko complex. Chet, the specialist in underground navigation, would have come in handy here—it was a damned shame about Chet—but Nick was fully prepared to carry on. Then the mission would be over. Hawk had said something about being on the lookout for little blue men or something equally bizarre, but Nick doubted that he would run into any during his infiltration mission. If he did, he grinned to himself, he would trap one with a saucer of milk and turn it over to the Air Force for study.

On silent feet he continued to prowl toward the reactor area, stopping only to make careful compass readings and note them on paper when he changed course. And it was during one of these short stops that Nick found the film box.

It had been tossed carelessly to the side, a popular brand of European film. He picked it up and examined it under the infrared light. The information on the wrapper

27

showed that it was a very high speed, fairly fine grain film, available only to professional photographers and laboratories. A wolfish grin split his features. Honest working men don't carry cameras on the job at top secret military installations.

Nick Carter wasn't the only unauthorized individual in the vast ventilating system. This knowledge caused him to drop his plans to reach the atomic reactor. There was a livelier game to play. It took him forty-five minutes to make a thorough check of the area.

His mental map of the route told him that this area was a barren section of the Musko complex. Drilling had been going on for a mammoth elevator system that would permit the Swedes to bring to the surface a whole flight of interceptor aircraft at one time. The project had been canceled when the location had been given away to the Russians and the interceptor squadron had been moved to another area where the Russians wouldn't know the location. There *should* be nothing for a spy here.

But suddenly his sixth sense, the life-preserving instinct which every hunting animal develops, warned him that the corridor was not empty long before his ears picked up the slight rasp of stealthy footsteps.

A workman, perhaps? Not likely. The beautifully balanced stiletto, Hugo, appeared in Nick's hand as if by magic.

The intruder was around a corner, not far away in the distance but perhaps long minutes in the labyrinth of the ventilating system. Nick began his stalk, two hundred pounds plus moving as delicately as a dancer. No careless footfall ever gave warning of Killmaster's approach.

Nick could hear the man ahead of him. Around one more corner, he judged, although sound could be deceptive in this maze. Whoever it was in front of him, and Nick was almost sure that he would turn out to be Chinese, the man was making an awful lot of noise. As if he were sure that he had eluded detection. Nick tightened his grip on the stiletto. The intruder didn't have to die.

That would all depend on the strength of his resistance and his readiness to answer questions.

The man was very close now, the rasping of his breath was loud in the corridor. Nick stepped noiselessly around the corner and flashed the infrared light toward his victim. It showed nothing.

The converging lines of the walls reached a vanishing point in the distance as empty as a surrealist landscape. The man had disappeared, entirely. Nick poised, tense to react against attack. All was stillness. The man had been swallowed up by the tunnel.

"Nuts," said Killmaster softly. He concentrated like a hunting animal but heard only the whispering air currents making their mechanical journey from point to point as they moved about the tunnel.

Then Nick saw the door, saw where it came away from the rest of the plating. Doors were made to be opened. Quietly he eased it open and flashed the dark light inside.

It was another tunnel cut out of granite, leading into the blackness of the island. Beyond that there was nothing. It was the shaftway, Nick guessed, that led to the abandoned aircraft launching site. Down it had passed the man Nick had just been stalking. Killmaster followed.

Before he stepped through the door he realized his mistake. He had assumed that any other of the opposition would make as much noise approaching as had the first one and Nick would have heard him coming. His mind was on his objective and he had left his rear unguarded. It was the sort of oversight that usually got a man killed.

The second man had been moving with quiet carelessness. He was as surprised as Nick when he came around the corner and caught the big American squarely in the beam of his flash. Nick heard the man grunt with surprise. Nick couldn't risk shooting. The shot would bring Flashlight's companions who would hunt him down through the labyrinth of the vents which they must know like the backs of their hands.

Grasping the stiletto, he sprang like a jaguar at the light. The two men hit the ground together making the sheet iron vent ring like a kettle drum crescendo. The man had a knife too and seemed to want silence as badly as Nick. N3 found out about the knife the hard way as he felt its painful kiss over the back of his left shoulder. Then Hugo was probing the defenses of the writhing man beneath him, bone cracked against bone and then, with quick expertise, Nick slid the stiletto into the man.

Beneath him the man stiffened.

"*Gross Gott* . . ." The man's breath exhaled in terror, and Nick clapped a hard hand over the gaping mouth to cut off the terminal scream of agony or supplication. When he pulled it away his hand was wet with blood. He rose and played the dark light down over the corpse.

A Kraut, thought N3—knock me down with an Iron Cross. His brief search of the body revealed little. The man was a piece in a crossword puzzle, nothing more. Nick left him where he lay and opened the door in the vent once more.

The unfinished sealed-off tunnel was of bare rock and two or three hundred feet across. A little moisture clung to the walls and without ventilation the air was dead and dank. Nick followed the slope down for several hundred yards and came out on a level plateau. Lights glowed from below the lip of the plateau. Using the dark light he moved cautiously toward the edge.

A hundred feet below, on the floor of the perpendicular shaft, was what looked like an encampment of gypsies. Or perhaps it looked like an encampment on the moon of some earthly expeditionary force. Equipment was set up beneath the blasted shards of rock that hung from the shaft wall. Half a dozen men reclined in sleeping bags or busied themselves at various technical jobs or worked over the drafting tables.

Nick lay on the ledge for some time noting details. He made no move to draw closer or interfere. This was Sweden's problem. He would report it to Vice Admiral

Larson at Swedish security but beyond that Nick had no desire nor authority to interfere in what shaped up as a major hassle between Sweden and one or the other of the Germanies. Also there was that dead guy in the vent to be reckoned with. If another one of these cave dwellers stumbled across him, Nick was in big trouble.

No, he would have to go back although it hurt Killmaster's professional instincts to leave something like this uninvestigated. But back he went. For once in his life he was going to err on the side of discretion. Hawk would have been pleased.

So it wasn't Nick's fault. He was on his way to do the right thing when he found out that it was too late. Nick heard the man coming down the tunnel, running, excited, but there was no place to hide. Then Nick was framed in a flashlight beam. He hurled himself to the granite floor of the tunnel and a bullet whizzed over his head, making a high buzzing sound as it ricocheted off the stone walls. Instantly Nick turned and worked his way back toward the ledge. The experience that he had gained in a hundred fights in cluttered darkened alleys from Argentina to Zambesi told him that if he stayed in the tunnel he was washed up.

He catfooted out on the ledge. A spotlight flitted from point to point on the wall like an angry bat. Nick's Luger spoke once, racketing off the walls of the cave and the light cut to a glow, then faded to nothing.

Far below him Nick heard commands rapped out in guttural German. The man in the air-conditioning shaft sent two more shots whining down the tunnel and Nick was forced far out on the edge of the ledge.

More lights went on below him—flashlights that could be turned on and off so he couldn't take aim—stung him with their beams like dogs baiting a mountain lion. As each light fell on Nick he sent a shot winging after it, but another light picked him up from another angle and as he turned for *that* light it too went out before he could fire and a third light picked him up. The bullets whined around him on the ledge like a swarm of angry bees whose sting meant death.

Nick decided it was getting just a little hot up there. He struggled toward the ladder that led down to the floor of the shaft. His hands caught the cold metal rungs and he swung himself over. He was taking a terrible chance. He was giving them his back as an easy target while he went down the ladder. Perhaps he could make it just a bit difficult though. He'd have to. He was badly outgunned and there wasn't a chance in a thousand that the noise of the guns in this sealed-off shaft would bring Swedish Security to his rescue.

More commands were shouted in German and he heard the men being deployed in the dark, their footsteps scraping like the scampering of mice over a stone floor. Deadly little mice, they were.

He started down the ladder with the bullets keening their little song of death around his ears. Down he went like a lumberjack in a speed contest, a bounding, joint-tearing descent that was second thing only to free fall— two rungs, three, four and five rungs at a time, catching hold of the ladder only long enough to break himself from plunging all the way to the granite floor.

Halfway down the cavern became flooded with light and the groundfire became more accurate. Even so Nick was moving too fast to be brought down by anything but a sharpshooter with all his wits about him. He dropped the last fifteen feet and hit the ground so hard that the shock almost blacked him out. Then he was rolling across the loose shale of the cavern's floor returning their fire, its echoes rolling off the walls in long angry swells. The gunfire became more rapid and less accurate. The German gunmen were beginning to panic as the notion struck them that this werewolf who had dropped among them might not die that night.

Nick charged the nearest gun, saw it wink white-blue twice, then the Luger in his hand bucked once and the man in front of him came to his feet clutching his chest only to topple over dead.

Nick went after the next gun the same way. At the last minute the German broke and ran and Nick shot him in the back because he was still armed and dangerous.

It was like an artist's recreation of war in the twenty-third century. Under the dead fluorescent lighting the German infiltrators clung to the sharp outcroppings of rock and fired at the American agent from half a dozen angles. Nick moved among them like an agent of death—a mad dog that couldn't be killed—returning their fire with twice their accuracy, flushing them out of their hiding places to be killed.

"*Achtung*," he screamed in a hoarse, angry voice that he didn't recognize. "Surrender or I will kill you one by one. Throw down those guns, *schnell*."

No guns were tossed down but, bit by bit, a silence fell over the cavern. Nick repeated his demand for surrender. No shots answered him and no one stepped forward waving his handkerchief. Nick grew uneasy. Perhaps they were short on ammunition and waiting for reinforcements. The tension of a man who suspects a trap but can't see it began to creep over him as the lust of battle receded.

The cavern was still. Not a pebble scraped in that desolate scene. The silence began to tell on Nick's nerves.

"What the hell," he said. Then he broke out of his cover and ran in short zigzag bursts toward the next rock. No shots. No nothing. Nick moved again. The cavern seemed empty and airless as the moon itself.

With infinite stealth Nick moved toward the rock where he knew a man with a Mauser lay concealed. He came upon the man and stopped in surprise. No shot of Nick's had harmed him but the man lay with his face against the rock, dead.

Nick turned the body over. It turned with the reluctance of dead weight common to the very drunk and the very dead. The man's face was pale, the eyes slightly protruding and the tendons of the neck taut. Nick cast the body aside and went on to the next. That man too was dead, and his symptoms were identical. Nick began to move faster and faster, running from one body to the next like a miser who has been robbed, glancing at each body and running to the next one. Killmaster had been cheated of his prey.

He was alone in the cavern with half a dozen spies who would not be interrogated now by anyone. The gray-clad figures about him lay limply like the last scene of a Greek tragedy, their dead forms seeming to accuse him some-how. Look, they said, see how easy it is, no more interrogations, no more reports; the ball's in your court now, baby. Good luck, you'll need it.

"God damn," Nick said. All of them at once, he thought, suicide by the numbers. It was weird and this damned futurama of a cavern didn't help any either.

Someone moaned, as weakly as a kitten. Nick sprang toward the noise and turned over the body. The face that stared back at him was young, handsome and blond. Nick looked at the body carefully. The man was wearing the uniform of the Wehrmacht without any insignia.

Long lashes fluttered and he moaned again. He was little more than a kid—pretty badly banged up. Probably fell from one of the ledges dodging bullets and hadn't had time to take the suicide pill. Lung shot, Nick noted dispassionately. Blood trickling out the corner of his mouth. Probably fatal.

Nick noticed the trooper had a bad bruise on the side of his head. He opened the collar of the tunic and slapped the man's face sharply. The German moaned louder and opened his eyes. The blue eyes focused on Nick and widened in terror. Then, with surprising strength, the young man galvanized into action and began to crawl away across the rocks. Nick caught him and thrust him over on his back with little effort.

The man's mouth worked and immediately his hand slipped to his mouth. At the last moment Nick saw a gleam of triumph light the blue eyes and he remembered the dead hanging from the rocks. Nick's fist drove into the man's solar plexus with the power of a mule's kick. The man doubled up and exhaled sharply. A small colorless pill flew out of his mouth and rolled among the stones. Nick ground it to dust with his heel.

"*Jawohl*," Nick said and slid the bright blade of the stiletto out into the light where the German could see it. A thin smile appeared on his face but his eyes did not smile. His face became a ghastly death's head that smiled and smiled with no humor at all.

"So," Nick said lovingly, "there is a time to live and a time to die and no death until I choose to give it to you. No cyanide but steel enough. I will enjoy this."

It was not the truth. Nick looked with strong distaste upon torture but playing the part of the psychopath frequently made the prisoner that much more nervous and anxious to talk. And Nick was not called Killmaster because he was squeamish.

"*Nein*," the young German gasped. "I vil nefer talk."

Twenty minutes later he was talking up a storm. Or talking as much as his wounds would let him. Nick had used the knife sparingly for the German was slipping fast and knew it. *In extremis* he wanted to talk, boast actually. Nick let him run on.

The flow of words became incoherent, stopped and started in different directions. He talked of his family, his studies. Nick had seen enough dying men to know that this one had a very limited amount of time before death stilled his tongue and there was a lot Nick wanted to know.

"What is the uniform you wear without insignia?" Nick demanded. The slur on his organization reached the German. The flow of words began again.

"The world belongs to the few, the very few who can manage . . . Goering, Hitler and that bunch . . . bunglers . . . all of them. . . ."

He paused and Nick thought for a moment that he had slipped off altogether. Then the blue eyes opened once more and the thick sensuous lips that contrasted so oddly with the strong arrogant face stretched in a smile.

"Ah, but the Teutonic Knights . . . they are a different breed. . . . The leadership of a man like Count von Stadee . . . twice the man Hitler could hope to be. Brilliant . . . allies . . . Republic of China. . . . We vil get America too." The man was babbling now, one word in ten was audible.

The man closed his eyes. Death was very close.

"What are you doing here in Sweden?" Nick rasped. The man laughed a little. Nick had to lean very close to hear his answer.

"Making money, of course. I'm a spectroscopic analyst. . . . A great joke, ja?"

Then he died and Nick was the only man left alive in the cave. Except perhaps for the joker who had pinned him down from the air-ventilator shaft. Nick had heard nothing from him for some time. By now he was probably at Stockholm airport buying his ticket for Berlin.

Nick looked at his dead prisoner. Another amateur with more ardor than common sense. He had just wanted to be allowed to play with the big boys and now look what had happened. Had he been kidding about being a scientist? Surveyors and military experts to analyze the underground defenses Nick could understand but lab boys were a mystery.

German neo-Nazism was a recurring nightmare haunting Europe. From here it looked a lot more tangible than a bad dream. This setup had taken serious dough and organization—it was far from the bellowing of juiced-up undergraduates at the German universities. There was something very big behind all this. Nick decided that he would be probably meeting Count von Stadee on a professional visit very soon.

CHAPTER 4

NICK'S FOOTSTEPS echoed somberly as he followed the thin bald head of the wizened little party who ran this way station of the dead.

The morgue looked like—well a morgue, Nick thought. There was nothing like it to compare it with. He heartily hoped when he went out it would be "lost in action" or "crashed and burned," instead of laid out naked on a refrigerated slab in the bowels of some public building with a ticket guessing who he might be tied to his toe.

"Yer say it was five oh three B yer wanted, mister?" the attendant whined. He stopped and squinted at the pass in his hand.

"That's right," Nick said. "Vice Admiral Larson sent me down."

"That's what I thought yer said. An' I don't care if St. Peter or the Queen o' Sheba sent yer down I ain't going near that particular stiff. Bright blue 'e is, mister. It don't pay to take chances in my business."

"Oh, Christ," Nick said tiredly, "I'll be all day down here looking for him. His name is Knudson. He came in this morning."

"I know. I know. Secret Service boys brought 'im in. Some kind o' scientist workin' with . . ." he stopped and groped for a phenomenon sufficiently hideous, ". . . with 'lectricity."

"Would fifty kroner be enough insulation?" Nick grinned.

"Not twenty million kroner, mister. Yer goin' on by yerself or not at all."

Nick was rarely the man to admit defeat but he knew he was licked.

37

"All right," Nick said wearily. "Which way to guest five oh three B and don't tell me I can't get there from here."

"Turn left at the end of the corridor, take the third door on yer left."

"Thanks," Nick said. He went on down the corridor whistling tunelessly between his teeth.

"An' don't come near me on yer way back, mister," the voice of the morgue attendant echoed after him. With some wrong turnings on the way Nick found his man. He would have been hard to miss. The dead body of Knudson stood out in contrast to the rest like some absurd genetic foulup. Nick couldn't blame the attendant much. He shivered himself, not from sensitivity but cold—the room was refrigerated and the temperature change was noticeable.

Overcoming his own distaste, Nick walked up to the table on which Knudson lay. The autopsy had been a complete failure. The examining physician's report had read: "Cause of death unknown." Possibly because the doctor wanted to get it over with as soon as possible he had been barely persuaded to refrain from adding: "Probably due to saturation with indigo rays in connection with experimental work on artificial electro-magnetic masses." That would have been all the scientific press of the world needed. The experiments would stop right there.

Nick's eyes roved up and down the body. It was closer now to black than blue.

His mind went back over what Swedish Security had told him about the circumstances of Knudson's death. Nick knew nothing about indigo emission rays but he knew a lot about the more violent causes of death.

He reached out tentatively and turned the body over. Then he ran his hands over the back of the dead man's head. There was no blood but his fingers found a spot at the base of the skull which was soft and pulpy. He whistled softly. Nick had been coshed often enough over the years to know the symptoms of *that*.

The scientist might have died of a mysterious emission

ray but first he had been the victim of a good old-fashioned sapping before he turned blue. Nick's lips turned back in a tight hardboiled grin.

It made him feel better to know that he had served some purpose in this science fiction world of the twentieth century.

Nick lit a cigarette and tried to think of the implications in this last piece of knowledge. For the German infiltration of the Musko defenses was suddenly very much his baby. His dreams of a Scandinavian holiday were a thing of the past. A brief talk with Hawk in Washington had taken care of that. It was no longer just Sweden's problem, Hawk informed him in a brief telephone conversation that went like this:

Hawk: (silkily) "So you thought you'd do a little spring skiing, Carter?"

NC: (casually) "It did cross my mind. Infiltration is Sweden's problem, isn't it?"

(static and flip on the picture tube)

Hawk: "I don't care if it's Martians who are selling secrets about the Milky Way to the Chicoms—anything Peking wants to know about, I want to know about too. You think the Chicoms are really interested in Sweden?"

NC: "Could be, chief."

Hawk: "Nuts, it's our underground defense systems they want to crack. You follow up what you've got. If the Swedes are working on a way to defend underground installations, I want them to find it."

NC: "Yes sir. That all?"

Hawk: "Yes. No, one other thing. Stay away from the booze and blondes."

Nick turned. Staring at the blue body of the scientist provided little inspiration.

But before he reached the door, the light went out and the room was plunged into profound blackness. Silent as the darkness itself Nick moved toward the door, a great heavy insulated thing. Nick put his weight against it once. It was locked. Nothing short of a bazooka would blast it open.

Inside he crouched in the dark waiting for an attack that never came. The silence grew thick and heavy. Who, he wondered, besides Vice Admiral Larson knew he was here and why he had come. Probably half of Swedish Intelligence from the typist pool on up, if office gossip and speculation were the same in Sweden as in the U.S. Government service. Then in the glimmer of light that filtered through from a crack where the refrigeration pipes ran out through the wall, Nick saw a man move.

Nick covered the distance between them in three silent gliding steps, the stiletto poised for action. The man seemed poised, listening. Nick took advantage of his lack of motion by lashing out with one hand and driving back the chin to leave the throat exposed. With his free hand Nick jabbed the needle point against the man's windpipe. The man in the dark didn't move a muscle.

He was already dead. A wave of reaction flooded through Nick and he chuckled without much humor. The joke was on him. Rigor mortis had peculiar characteristics sometimes. A change of temperature or something internal could relax or tighten a muscle and make a dead man move.

Nick went back to his waiting game. The air was becoming thick and bad. He checked his watch. It was late in the day and no one was expecting him anywhere until tomorrow morning.

He lay down on the floor and the air was a trifle better there, but not much. He wondered how much air the room held. Not a great deal. It wasn't very big. Minutes later he was having trouble breathing and at the same time getting very drowsy. The hard cement floor was beginning to feel as soft as a bed. The cold stone felt so comfortable against his cheek he promised himself a half hour's cat nap before deciding what to do about the situation. What are they trying to do, he thought drowsily, frighten me to death?

But the knowledge of danger stayed with him, spurred him on. He couldn't let them win as easily as that. With infinite weariness Nick climbed to his feet. That crack where the chink of light was coming in. There would be fresh air there. Perhaps just enough for a mouse but it was better than nothing. With the remnants of his strength he shoved one of the corpses from its table with a muttered apology and dragged the table over near the pipes. The table wasn't high enough for him to reach the chink. With much stumbling and effort Nick turned the table on its end and climbed precariously on top of it. By stretching full length he managed to get his face up to the chink.

The tiny current of fresh air revived him a little. Nick put his mouth to the chink and roared.

"Hey, you God damned jarhead Swedes. You incomparable ignoramuses, let me the hell out of here."

His shouting echoed down the short empty hall with no effect whatsoever. Nick continued until he ran so short of breath he risked falling from his shaky perch.

Hours passed. Nick's legs became so shaky they threatened to drop him off the table and he knew if that happened he wouldn't have the strength to climb back up. So he hung on grimly. They had almost got Killmaster this time by the simplest of tricks but by God "almost" wasn't good enough. He was going to hang onto that damned pipe until he was rusted to it.

The hours became a timeless period of agony that dissolved into a meaningless ache. His brain was aching from the complaints from his legs. Then he heard the door open. He let go of the pipe and dove toward the open door. The table came crashing down like the crack of doom.

The white-coated morgue attendant flattened himself against the wall with a gasp of horror as the huge man appeared out of the darkness, stumbling toward him on rubbery legs like some updated version of Frankenstein's monster.

"Oh, no-o-o," he screamed with the drawn-out cry of someone who has seen the unseeable. Nick caught his throat and hoisted the little man halfway up the wall and delivered himself of some off-the-cuff remarks about morgue attendants who failed to keep an eye on dangerous places like refrigerated rooms.

"Sir, sir . . ." the little one gasped. "I have just come on duty, only ten minutes ago. The four-o'clock man went home sick."

Nick took his face out of the little man's face in order to see him better. The statement just might be true. Obviously this attendant was not the little old cadaver who had let him in.

The new man was a dapper little fellow with the slightly popeyed gaze of a man suffering from a thyroid condition. Right now his eyes looked like bull's eyes, as if he couldn't rid himself of the notion that some foe had come back from the grave to pay an old debt.

Nick slowly eased the man to the floor, keeping hold of him with one huge hand. The morgue attendant stared back at the furious American in fear and trembling.

"You sure you didn't come back to find out if I was dead yet?" Nick growled.

"Oh, no, sir. I've been with the city for twenty years. You can check. Besides, I love Americans. I speak English real goot," Popeye said slipping into the vernacular. "Yes siree, bob. Some good, huh? Listen, let me take ya down to the dispensary, kid. We'll have you lookin' like the cat's pajamas in no time."

Nick released the man reluctantly. If this was a neo-Nazi, the movement could use help.

"Never mind," Nick said. "Don't go far from your telephone, I may want to talk to you again."

"Don't worry, pal," the round-faced little morgueman said. "I'm here Tuesday through Saturday every day. My home phone is twelve, forty-three, forty-six. I live at thirty-seven Vasagaten . . ."

"That's peachy," Nick said. He went off to telephone security and point out to Vice Admiral Larson that his office wasn't as secure as it might be.

Vice Admiral Larson was a cigar-chewing, mutton-chopped, whiskered Swede right out of another century. Now his seaman's blue eyes were cold and hard as he put down the conical-shaped receiver of his telephone.

"Musko Hospital tells me that they have no morgue attendant on night duty, Mr. Carter."

Nick lounged in a low leather chair in Larson's sumptuously appointed office of polished wood and stainless steel and jiggled the ice in his scotch.

"Then we not only have to find the guy who locked me in your damned morgue. We have to find the guy who let me out."

Larson poured himself a healthy shot of scotch from the bottle that was making rings on his magnificent desk top and drank it neat.

"That's going to be more difficult. He's gone and the real morgue attendant was admitted to Musko Hospital early this evening with severe lacerations and internal injuries. He died an hour ago."

"Oh," Nick said. He looked into the depths of his drink and wondered idly if the testy old codger was now laid out on a table next to Knudson.

"I've talked with your Mr. Hawk," Larson went on. "He wants you to continue on the case working loosely under my direction. He seems to feel that whoever is interested in cracking our defenses is really after your NORAD setup and atomic missile sites."

"Always that possibility, sir," Nick said.

The vice admiral grunted and put his feet up on the desk.

"Needless to say we're as embarrassed as hell about all this. Nevertheless we'll cooperate and be glad of the help."

The bearded Swedish Intelligence chief shoved the bottle toward Nick with the point of one toe.

"Have another drink, Carter. Then I'll fill you in on what we know about the Teutonic Knights. By the way, we've traced Count von Stadee to Copenhagen without

much difficulty. He travels with an entourage that would
be excessive even for a maharajah. . . . Now listen, I've
got a plan. It means you'll have to work with a woman,
which I know is a handicap, but you may like this one.
She's pretty bright and has a lot of nerve. She isn't too bad
looking considering she's the scientific type. . . ."

For some hours Larson talked with Nick listening and
asking questions.

Nick pulled the shiny new Mercedes convertible, one of
his new props, up in front of the house on the headland
and climbed the rough-beamed stairs that led up the hill-
side to the house. He was no longer Nick Carter, the
steely-eyed AXEman second only to Hawk himself. He
was now Nicholas von Runstadt, ex-Luftwaffe wing commander presently a soldier of fortune with a weakness for
dames and schnapps. He wore no disguise but he had
changed in a hundred different ways—his haircut, his
posture, his mannerisms, the cut of his clothes—he was
different enough to make it hard for even Hawk to recognize him.

On the porch Nick pressed the doorbell and heard
chimes within the house. He waited a period and rang
again. There was no answer. When the bell failed to
produce an answer at the fourth ring Nick began to get
worried.

Astrid Lundgren, from what Nick had heard, was a
dangerous obstacle to anyone interested in neutralizing the
Swedish underground defenses. And the Teutonic Knights
were obviously well organized and moved fast. Nick tried
the heavy wooden door once but wasted no time trying to
break it down. Instead he moved around to the window.
It was open and he stepped inside with one fluid motion.

It was quiet there with the oppressive silence of a house
which is empty or has just seen a fatal accident. Nick
moved quickly through the downstairs rooms calling the

woman's name. There was no answer. The upstairs too was empty.

It was the right house all right. Going through the library Nick had seen the heavily laden shelves of technical books by Einstein, Fermi, Oppenheimer and scores of other internationally famed physicists.

The back door was ajar. Nick stepped out onto a wooden sun deck.

A tall blonde woman with the sort of body most movie stars would like to have was toweling herself down after the rigors of a sauna treatment. Her tawny back was toward Nick and he stopped in awestruck admiration at the perfection of the sight. Her legs were long and shapely, her buttocks taut but ample and a river of white-blond hair cascaded down the rippling back.

Nick, entranced by the vision, brought himself back to reality remembering how little time he had to make his plane. He cleared his throat. The woman didn't seem to hear him. She reached for the shelf where her toilet articles lay and turned casually in his direction, still toweling herself.

Then a revolver went crack, crack, and Nick heard the bullets whack into the wood behind his head.

"That is just to show that I know how to use this gun," the woman said. She advanced toward him covering herself with the towel and keeping the gun leveled at his midriff.

Nick decided that she was even more spectacular from the front.

"I'm looking for Doctor Lundgren, dear," Nick said. "Perhaps you can tell me if she's at home."

"I'm Doctor Lundgren," she said. The sea-green eyes glittered suspiciously. "Who, pray tell, are you?"

Nick blinked. It was hard to believe that this woman had read all the books in the library and written a few of her own.

"Right now I'm Nicholas von Runstadt," Nick said.

"I'm the guy you were running away to Copenhagen with for the weekend, remember?"

"Oh, my God," she said grimly, "another pretty boy. Where in the world does Larson find them? American, aren't you?"

"Yes."

Her eyes were coolly appraising. "Don't believe everything you've heard about Swedish women. Not this one, anyway."

"I take nothing on hearsay," Nick grinned.

Her glance was disdainful. She slid into a bathrobe and they walked together toward the house, her footsteps leaving wet marks on the fitted floor of the sun deck.

"Don't get any bright ideas, my friend," she said. "This is strictly for King, country and the preservation of the species."

"Well, you'd better get a move on if you're going to save the human race today," Nick said. "Our plane leaves from Stockholm in two hours."

She turned to him her eyes wide.

"I thought it was tomorrow. I've been running linear acceleration variations on the same stuff for two days now. I don't even know what day it is."

Then the Swedish-modern version of the absent-minded professor went upstairs to pack and change. Nick sat in the library and thumbed through a draft paper titled "Observations and Speculations of the Activity of Semi-Charged Particles in the Musko Linear Accelerator." He understood one word in ten.

Out the window he could see sailboats well out past the forbidden zone. He wondered if Count von Stadee would accept his offer to turn Doctor Astrid Lundgren over to him for a mere five hundred thousand marks.

CHAPTER 5

THE HAWKER SIDDLEY twin jet took off from a private airfield in Bavaria and pointed its sleek nose north on a direct route toward Copenhagen.

By the time they were airborne for twenty minutes the Big Man himself felt good enough to come forward and take over the controls. Hans, the pilot, kept silent waiting to learn Count von Stadee's mood before risking conversation. Not too bad for a man who has lost five million dollars in one afternoon, Hans finally decided.

Hans was a great, gruff, ex-Luftwaffe pilot, a famous beer drinker and possessor of a spurious heartiness that passed as good humor. As such he reigned as sort of court fool to von Stadee and was permitted slight liberties that the Count would ruin other men for even daring.

"We will be in Denmark in time for the dance, I see," von Stadee observed. "Two more hours at this speed. I will have time to return to the hotel."

"Not exactly, chief," Hans said cautiously. "You remember the airspeed isn't the same as speed over the ground. We have a pretty good headwind blowing from out of the north—"

"Yes of course," the Count said stiffly. "I was mistaken. Foolish of me."

Hans shut his mouth. The boss didn't like to be caught out. The Count's thin drawn face was set in hard lines. Hans could even hear the noise of his teeth grinding. Brilliant but too damned nervous was Hans' diagnosis. The man would rule the world or die of strain inside of five years. Three times on the cover of *Der Spiegel* ... flying two or three times across Germany in a single day to address this industrial club or that convention ... his multi-million-dollar drug industry had been mentioned by none other than ex-Chancelor Ehrhardt as a prime mover in the early days of the "Economic Miracle." Von Stadee called the powers of the Ruhr by their nicknames, sat on the board of five major banks and at the same time kept up with his surgical practice. Hans knew a little something about that surgical practice as he knew a great many other things that the Count didn't suppose he knew.

The radio crackled, breaking the silence of the cockpit.

"It's home, boss," Hans said. He pushed the talk button and said go ahead.

"Copenhagen reports von Runstadt and Lundgren under observation. States that they have arrived safely in Copenhagen and were under routine surveillance by Swedish Security men until this afternoon but von Rundstadt has now managed to avoid the Swedish surveillance. Appears that he is planning to keep tonight's rendezvous and will be able to deliver the woman."

"Very good," von Stadee said. "That will be all."

The radio went dead.

"Damn lucky thing about circulating the reward for the Lundgren dame, boss," Hans observed. "I thought we were out five million when that Swedish operation blew out on us."

Von Stadee's voice was silky. "Does it ever occur to you, Hans, to ask yourself why you are still no more than an airplane driver after thirty years? No? Let me suggest some reasons. One, these petty criminals, which is what this von Runstadt seems to amount to, however glorious his war records were, are involved in a foolish and risky business. A last resort. Secondly, our allies who are presently the Chinese would much prefer for us to have given them the secret of Musko without anyone knowing we were looking for it, so that their use of it against the United States would contain more of the element of surprise. And finally, because if you really had your ear to the ground you'd know that I canceled that Swedish business three days ago and the fools in the cave wasted time getting out. They would have been shot by me when they returned in any event. Now be so kind as to take over the controls. I have some business with our friend Lin-Tao. Finally, let me inform you that what is essentially the mastery of North America I am not selling for a mere five million."

"I should have known, chief," Hans said, flushing and chomping the butt of his cigar. "You're always one jump ahead of the rest of us."

After the Count went back Hans' small eyes were furrowed in thought, a form of pain that he seldom endured. He knew the Count was lying about having ordered the Musko infiltrators home. He had been caught with his pants down like any normal man. Lying was hardly repugnant to Hans but as indication of change it worried him. He had never caught the Count telling anything but the strictest truth! Of course that and the boasting might have been merely to make up for the miscalculating of the airspeed but some instinct told the corpulent pilot that a lie meant loss of control. Hans had seen it happen before. After that always seemed to come a kind of Armageddon. His little eyes brightened. When the mighty fell a lot of noise was made by their going but there were usually fine pickings for the unobtrusive ones who were on the spot.

The fir-clad Jutland Peninsula appeared below the wing. Hans corrected his heading slightly and began his descent into Copenhagen.

It was a dark land and strangely lighted. Its people were a strange and graceful race, moving to the rhythms of music that conjured up semi-enchanted forests and rushing streams. The Royal Danish Ballet had been in full swing for over half an hour when the party entered the darkened box that Nick had been occupying in solitary splendor since the beginning of the performance. Nick nodded toward the group and returned his attention to the dance. Von Runstadt, he had decided, was an aristocrat and played it cool. Only when the lights went up at intermission did Nick turn and face the group in the box.

He had no trouble picking out von Stadee. The rest of the hangers-on looked like hangers-on to a big man anywhere, their faces bland and revealing various degrees of crookedness and assumed dignity. But von Stadee was a surprise. Nick had been looking for the stereotyped die-hard Nazi—the cropped head, the bull neck, the Prussian stiffness, perhaps going a little to fat.

The elegant man in evening clothes looked like a cross between a Marine field commander and an El Greco saint. He was strong, Nick realized, much stronger than his slimness would show, and his face beneath the gray crew cut was all-weathered good health like an outdoor man's, though the eyes were hollow and burned brightly as a man with fever.

The Count finished saying something to his female companion and turned to Nick.

"Good evening, Herr von Runstadt. I am so glad that you were able to take advantage of my offer. But I sent you two tickets and you are alone."

His cultivated voice was just unable to conceal an edge of scorn.

"I left the fräulein home," Nick said bluntly. "I thought it best that she be absent while we haggle over her."

Von Stadee laughed depreciatingly.

"My dear chap, I never haggle. You have been informed of the price which you may take or leave. It is a pity, however, that the good Dr. Lundgren isn't with us tonight because I am always reluctant to buy a pig in a poke so to speak."

"Pig in a poke, hell," Nick snorted. "I know what the Lundgren woman is worth to you."

"Do you really?" von Stadee breathed. "How very interesting."

"Yes," Nick went on, "and I know she's worth a damn

sight more than the five hundred thousand Deutschemarks you're offering for her."

"Just how much more?" von Stadee asked softly. Nick would have had to be a very stupid man not to realize the danger in the voice.

"I'm not a greedy man, Count," Nick said rather over-heartily. "I don't want money. But when Sweden discovers that she's missing they'll be after me like the hounds of hell and so will the rest of the NATO countries, including West Germany. I'll be a man without a future, Count. In any case it is difficult now for a patriotic German . . ."

"Yes," said von Stadee, making it come out something between an affirmation and a question.

"I want a job with your organization. Obviously you can use a good man and I've held rank in half a dozen armies."

The Count shook his head. "I've told you that you will be well protected. I have gone to considerable expense and trouble to see that the woman is convincingly kidnapped from you. Shortly thereafter she will turn up dead. None of this will be your fault."

"I still want the job. No job, no Swedish fräulein," Nick said.

There was silence while the Count lowered his eyes and thought. Nick's gaze was attracted by the woman sitting next to the Count. She seemed incredibly young to be the Count's mistress. He was in his early forties while she couldn't have been a day over twenty. She was an odd one for the Count anyway. She had the pert face, creamy white skin and the very dark hair of some Irish girls Nick had known. Nick winked at her and concealed a grin. The Count wasn't thinking anything over any more than Nick was haggling. They both knew what the payoff was to be but they both were forced to act out the charade.

Nick used the interlude to pull a silver flask out of his jacket and gallantly offered the girl the first drink. Her dark blue eyes twinkled briefly.

"Thanks, sure," she said. "I mean *danke schön*."

I'll be damned, Nick thought, *an American.*

Von Stadee looked up disapprovingly as the girl handed the flask back to Nick. Nick offered the flask to the Count who shook his head curtly. Nick shrugged and took a giant swallow.

"Always comes in handy against life's little vicissitudes, is what I always say," Nick said sententiously and grinned boorishly.

"I have come to a decision," the Count said, ignoring him. "It is possible that we can use a man of your experience in our political organization. However, even I cannot bend the rules of admittance. I will support your candidacy but you will have to pass the requirements as you would for any other business or military organization. Some of them are a little out of the ordinary but so too are the Teutonic Knights, at least at the level of paid officers."

"I understand," Nick said. He did to a point. Right now, von Stadee would have just as earnestly promised to bring him a bucketful of shooting stars.

Von Stadee drew an envelope from the pocket of his jacket and handed it to Nick.

"The plans for the prisoner exchange are written on a piece of paper which will disintegrate before you leave this box. Study them and if you have any questions, ask me now. I will expect no mistakes tomorrow night."

Nick read the simple instructions over three times until he had them word perfect and then looked up.

"No questions."

Von Stadee nodded approvingly and handed him another envelope. Nick counted the *Judas Gelt* and it was his turn to nod.

"One last thing," von Stadee said. "I think it would be best if all of us were to remain around Copenhagen for a while to avoid the . . . er appearance of evil-doing. The evidence will point away from both of us so there will be no need to fear the authorities."

Nick agreed. When von Stadee's party left Nick remained behind and left by another entrance. The Count would probably have posted someone to watch Nick and be sure that he behaved like a conspirator and Nick believed in giving service for value received.

Copenhagen was at its springlike best, all cobbled street, brick buildings and picturesque quais. God help Astrid, Nick thought to himself, if you blow this one. He remembered the full wet lips of the Count and his burning eyes. Oh, yes, if that old boy gets hold of you, Astrid dear, you'll talk and talk and talk.

The pictures in Nick's imagination were not pretty as he walked through the girl-filled streets of Copenhagen back to the hotel. The goddess was asleep when he got there. Her protector undressed with a wry chuckle and slid chastely into the other bed, true to his deal with her.

Eight P.M. and the dwarf spun the wheel. The wheel whirled and whirled and sent its lights spinning up into the night to merge with the kaleidoscope of lights that flitted through the trees.

The music was the weird monotony of the steam calliope.

The dwarf called, "Step right up, ladies and gentlemen, see them all . . . all the stars."

Down by the shore an orchestra was playing. In fact, half a dozen were playing slow waltzes, hot Dixieland and rock'n roll for the ye-ye-bunch.

"Frank Sinatra, folks . . . Yves Montand . . . Louis Armstrong . . . Nureyev . . . all ready to perform for you for a fraction of their normal price."

But the stars were puppets and the dwarf couldn't have sold the Beatles live and in person that night. It was raining and the dwarf had a bad corner. No one bought a ticket to sit in the unroofed fenced-in area in front of the puppet stand.

A tall man and a woman in a raincoat stood off among the trees just far enough away so that the dwarf couldn't importune them to see his show.

The dwarf shielded his cigar against the rain and went through his spiel from time to time with glazed eyes.

The rain dripped tiredly from the freshly opened leaves.

Eight o'clock. Any minute now. Nick stood very close to the girl. It was very romantic that way. It was also much safer. Up close to Astrid like that, they couldn't cut him down from ambush without risking killing her which was about the one risk von Stadee wouldn't be prepared to take. Nick had just one job tonight. Stay alive.

There was a drop of water on the tip of Astrid's nose. Nick kissed it off. It gave him the chance to touch her body and check the infinitesimal high frequency radio receiver with which the Swedish Security would be able to follow her every movement in case something went wrong.

Of course there was always the long shot chance that von Stadee would honor his promise to Nick instead of trying to kill him, but Nick personally thought it was unlikely. He would have respected the Count a great deal less if the Count hadn't made arrangements to have Nick bumped off.

"How you doing?" Nick asked.

"Fine. No. I'm frightened. I've led a very sheltered life."

"I'll say," Nick grinned. "Seriously, Admiral Larson and his blokes will have you safe and sound even if I'm too busy to be much help."

"I'd rather have you," the girl said in her throaty voice. "All things considered."

"I told you I grow on you," Nick grinned.

The dwarf was starting up his spiel again. "Come and see the stars, folks. . . . They're all here, an international galaxy of the famed and talented." His hoarse voice croaked on and on like a raven in the fog.

"There's a man with a taste for talent. Bring your lady up close, sir, and let her see another side of life."

The dwarf swung one of the stage spotlights around so

that it fell full on Nick. Nick didn't know whether it was tired whimsy or part of the plan. He felt Astrid stiffen beside him. Suddenly the misty park was full of running forms.

"I say," Nick bellowed. Outrage filled his voice. They were encircled and the men were lunging closer. The dwarf began to laugh, his cackling reaching an insane pitch. Nick hoped he wouldn't have to give the girl up. Swedish Security had the park ringed but, nevertheless, it would be safer if he could keep her and sell the Count on a second try.

A shot cracked out of the mist and the dwarf laughed harder. Nick saw more red tongues of flame, heard more shots but he was already on the soaking grass and his Luger was clear and trembling in his hand as it roared back defiance. A wounded man groaned. Astrid was up close against Nick, one long leg thrown over his, and her hair blew in his eyes as he tried to find the misty outlines of the kidnapers in his sights.

"Let's get out of here," he growled to Astrid.

"Did I say I wanted to stay?" she said into his ear.

Nick pulled her to her feet with one hand, keeping the Luger firing with the other. Together they dashed for the protection of the trees. A man with a gun appeared on the slippery path. Nick shot him just as he raised the weapon and Astrid screamed.

"One of the rules of the game, dear," Nick whispered. "We don't scream when we shoot or get shot. Gives away our position."

"I don't think I like this game too much."

Nick chuckled shortly. "Like the man said, right now it's the only game in town."

The boat rental at the little lake was deserted on this rainy night. Together Nick and Astrid ran down the dock and stepped into the nearest rowboat. Already they could hear the hue and cry being raised along the banks. Nick worked the oars, pulling hard for the misty obscurity of the middle of the lake.

CHAPTER 6

THE LIGHTS of the park glowed against the overcast night sky but on the lake the mist and rain enveloped them with a protective cloak of darkness. Nick and Astrid sat in silence, listening to the water lap against the boat. The noises of the park seemed far off and even the shouting of their pursuers along the shore seemed to be dwindling.

Then in the silence an oarlock creaked. Not one of theirs. They heard voices as boats glided out into the middle of the pond.

Nick put his hand on the girl's arm.

"Stay very quiet," Nick said. "No matter what happens."

She pushed back a stray lock of his dark hair that had fallen over his forehead.

"All right," she said, "I don't have to be told things twice. They're coming after us now?"

"Yes," Nick said.

"I can't hear them."

"Yes, you can," Nick whispered. "Off to the left. Get down behind the gunwales."

The girl pulled her skirt up and hunkered obediently in the leaky bottom of the rowboat. Nick took one of the oars out of its lock and sculled quietly, moving the boat toward the deeper darkness of the trees overhanging the bank. The sounds of the other boat were getting closer. Nick stripped off his clothes.

"Is that them, the Germans?" she whispered.

"I think so," Nick said. "It might also be the police about the German I killed on the path. I've got to find out."

56

He slid as silently as he could into the water but he could tell that the other boat had heard the splash and was now pulling directly toward them. Nick submerged and swam under water for some distance. When he came up the new boat was very close. It carried two men whispering excitedly in German.

"*Achtung*! There, Walter, ahead of us."

The man in the bow had a gun and was kneeling to get a better aim at the shadow that was Nick's boat.

"Be very careful not to hit the woman. She is valuable merchandise," the man at the oars whispered.

"This damn fog," the gunman said. "I can see the boat but not the man."

Nick exploded out of the black water and hurled his weight onto the prow of the rowboat.

"Hey, keep your damned weight in the middle, damned Silesian oaf—what—?"

The gunman concentrating on his aim was taken by surprise and catapulted over the bow into the water. The roar of the gun next to Nick's ear stunned him temporarily. In the hiatus the man at the oars tried to beat Nick's skull in with an oar. Nick felt the sharp blade crash numbingly down on his shoulder and drank half the pond trying to get out of the way. Then he caught hold of the oar and began to climb hand over hand. At first the oarsman was too stubborn or too stupid to let go and drop Nick back in the water.

When he finally got the idea it was too late. Nick caught hold of his neck with both hands and fell backwards into the water. The oarsman had to come along or let his head be torn off. They hit the water together and the pressure of Nick's fingers increased remorselessly on the man's throat.

While the man underwater struggled, Nick checked to the rear. The gunman was coming back, hampered by his clothing but full of fight. Nick saw his face, grimacing in the water beside him and released his hold on the rower's throat long enough to send a sharp, vicious backhand

chop into the gunman's face. The blade of Nick's hand
struck like the blunt edge of an axe, the blow timed
perfectly to drive the man's nose back up into his brain.
The man didn't even have time to scream. He was dead
before his ruined face sank into the blackness of the
water.

Nick returned his attention to the rower he was holding
under water. The man's struggles were becoming steadily
weaker. Nick tread water for two more full minutes, his
face an implacable mask, then he released his hold. The
second German failed to come up.

There'll be more, he thought. They must have us ringed
along the shore or they wouldn't risk men in a boat.
Nevertheless, now that they knew where he was he would
have to risk a landing. He swam thoughtfully back to his
own boat and pulled himself over the gunwales.

"I—I heard a gun shot only once," Astrid said. "I
thought maybe . . ."

"Maybe," Nick laughed, isn't good enough." He took
the oars and began to row hard toward the shore. As they
came up on the bank, each bush and tree trunk loomed
out of the mist like the shadow of a gunman. Nick ran the
boat well up on the bank and handed the girl out. Then
they ran up the slippery path into the dark of the
woods.

In the woods the mist cut visibility down to a few feet.
Up from the damp earth came the sharp fragrances of a
wet late spring and a knowledge of evil, clear and undi-
luted as few men ever know it.

The dwarf was laughing somewhere in those ferny
woods. Nick had heard that maniacal laughter only once,
minutes before at the puppet show, but it was etched into
his brain so deeply that he would hear it again twenty
years later on bad nights, if he lived that long. Perhaps the
laughter was some nervous manifestation of the blood lust
that would handicap the little killer always. He was out
there somewhere in the dark and laughing because he
knew where Nick was but Nick didn't know about him.

The girl gasped but true to her word she held her tongue. Her eyes were wide with fright and her hand was deathly cold as she gripped Nick's.

Doggedly he climbed the mud path with the girl behind, stubbornly asking for a bullet from the little obscenity crouching in ambush.

No bullet came but the laughter followed them like a bad spirit of the wood, flitting now ahead, now behind.

Then abruptly the laughter ceased.

Then Nick's supersensitive ears, tuned by years of night fighting, caught the click of iron on iron a moment before the laughter broke out ahead of him once more. Nick hurled the girl to the muddy path and dropped swiftly on top of her as the single red eye of a machine gun chattered its deadly fusillade a few yards up the trail. For what seemed like minutes on end the red death chattered out of the mists while Nick and Astrid ground their faces into the mud and tried to keep themselves small. Finally the reverberations died away and the beam of a flashlight played tentatively through the tendrils of the drifting fog.

Nick snapped off a shot with the Luger and heard the bullet ricochet off rocks. The light went out and the laughter started up again.

The girl beside him started to shake like a fever victim.

"That laughing," Astrid said, "it's awful. It frightens me more than the machine gun—more than death itself."

"I have an idea that's what it's supposed to do," Nick whispered laconically. "Stay here while I make a fast reconnaissance. Maybe we can dampen some of that good humor."

The grip of the Luger was damp and heavy in Nick's hand and he kept up a rapid fire in the direction of the dwarf's insane cackling to draw attention from Astrid. Ahead of him the machine gun's red tongue flickered like a moray eel defending its hole. Wet pieces of bark and torn leaves drifted down around Nick's head as the big man moved like a wraith after the retreating machine gunner. The dwarf was insane but he wasn't dumb. He knew by the speed with which Nick was moving up on him in the dark that he didn't stand a chance against the big man in a shootout over rough terrain. Soon the machine gun bursts came from farther and farther away. The dwarf was retreating fast. Quick little bastard, Nick noted. Obviously he hadn't figured on having to handle Nick alone. And he could be quiet when he had to be. Nick also noted that fact for further reference.

Well, there was no point stumbling around out here in the boondocks if Mr. Dwarf had had enough. The big thing was to keep Astrid Lundgren safe.

Nick was close enough to the path so that he should have heard any movement in Astrid's direction but he didn't take an easy breath until he saw her on his back trail clinging to a tree. He heard her sharp intake of breath as he appeared noiselessly beside her.

"Are we safe now?" she asked.

"For a couple of minutes," Nick grinned. "They sure must want you badly to take chances like this."

"They do," the girl said simply. "I do not boast. I am merely a pawn who blocks an important square and therefore a valuable commodity. The results to the free world would be drastic if I were lost. It is a fact."

"Von Stadee was lucky," Nick growled. "Without this fog we'd have had you safely home in Sweden by now."

Nick kept the Luger within easy reach as they walked up the hill toward the lights of the amusement park. A few hundred yards to go, Nick judged, to the safety of the street and the reinforcement of Admiral Larson's men. But until he got outside the walls Astrid was his grim responsibility. Well, big wins usually mean big risks. With any luck the risking part would soon be over.

They were approaching the amusement area now.

On this drizzly night the area was lightly attended but the few people there might serve to keep the gunplay down to a minimum. Within five minutes Nick spotted one of the Count's men sitting at a café table by himself, the only person outside—big, Teutonic and about as in-conspicious as the Brandenburg Gate. He caught sight of Nick almost at the same time and spoke rapidly into a walkie-talkie. Nick increased his pace, dragging the girl along by the hand. Half a dozen cropped-haired men in raincoats were coming for him down the midway.

It was too late. Of course the gate would have been most heavily guarded. If von Stadee had had sense enough to equip his thugs' guns with silencers, they could cut Nick down with a solid wall of fire without anyone notic-ing. Safety was reaching the Vesterbrogade, the great main street outside the gate a few hundred feet away, but Nick knew that they weren't going to make it.

He turned and started off the way he had come, throwing a glance over his shoulder. Von Stadee's six boy scouts were jogging along after him, coming steadily closer.

Three more were coming up the path the other way. The Count had Nick boxed in nicely. He might, just might, be able to fight his way out against eight men but never with the girl. Then Nick saw the airplane ride on his left just discharging its passengers. He pulled the panting girl around behind a flower vendor's stand and shoved a handful of kroner at the ticket taker.

The ticket taker was old and inclined toward conversa-tion.

"The seats are wet, sir. Perhaps you and your lady would come another night. We will be closing down soon. . . ."

"No, no thank you, my fiancée adores the ride." Nick grinned maniacally and yanked Astrid's hand. She forced herself to look enthusiastic. "Yes, indeed, how she loves the ride. Here give us half a dozen tickets."

Nick jammed the string of tickets into his pockets and raced for the gate. The attendant was dropping the bar, ready to start the ride. Nick and Astrid shoved their tickets into his hand and jammed through. The rest of the seats were taken by tow-headed Danish teenagers and a handful of Norwegian sailors, too drunk to find chippies on this wet night.

"Wh—what does this machine do?" Astrid said in a shaky voice. "Mechanically it looks most inefficient."

"Don't know," Nick said as he buckled them in. "Don't care." The rest of his words were lost in the roar of the music that went up as the machine started off abruptly and began to gain speed.

The airplane ride went higher than it seemed at first glance. Nick and Astrid went spinning up over the edge of the trees, caught glimpses of the lowering night sky over Copenhagen and then came swooping past the flashing lights of the ground. The music played wildly—"That Daring Young Man on the Flying Trapeze"—and the faces on the ground were a series of blurs as Nick tried to pick out the Count's black-raincoated killers.

The Norwegian seamen were bellowing with laughter. Below them Nick caught sight of the bunch of black coats with white faces staring up from the middle of the walk. He turned his head quickly.

The little metal capsule at the end of the iron arm gyrated wildly far over the ground. Nick saw the lights of traffic on Hans Christian Andersen Boulevard and then the ride was slowing down, coming to a halt.

The old ticket taker came out on the platform. People were getting out, more were getting into the little tin buckets. No. Yes. Two of the black raincoats were coming through the gate, lumbering down the wooden platform. There they made a mistake.

They greeted Nick and Astrid with guttural good cheer and tried to climb into the back seat of their little bucket. There were a lot of free buckets available.

"*Guten Tag, Herr von Runstadt,*" the big one said. "Ve take a little ride together, *ja*? Den you join mit us for schnapps, *ja*?"

Their guns were in their pockets for the moment. Nick grinned pleasantly and stood up in his seat. Then he drove his right fist into the big German's nose with all the power of his brawny back and shoulder behind it. The German's nose exploded like an overripe tomato and blood poured over his mouth and chin, staining his shirt collar and his black raincoat.

The German began a bubbling stream of curses that was cut off when the ride started with a lurch. The second German gunman grabbed his bleeding companion and shoved him into the tin gondola just as the ride started with a lurch.

Once again the machine carried them sailing through the night sky, twirling in a crazy orbit around its ancient engine. The wounded gunman groped for his gun, his ruined face working, his pulpy crimson lips drawn back to reveal snarling yellow teeth.

"Ve shoot him now, the svine . . ."

"Nonsense, Carl. You are an idiot. The point is to get away with the girl, not to hand us all over to the Danish police. Try to use that thick Bavarian head for something other than a punching bag."

"I kill him now und giff you a bullet too if you try to stop me, *ja*."

"The Count will have you hunted down like a dog," the second German said coolly. "Even you, Carl, are not too stupid to understand that. You will get your chance, never fear. Look, the ride is surrounded."

For the time being Nick had mentally divided the two raincoated killers into the Good German who preached caution and the Bad German who wanted to kill him now. The Good German was telling the truth. Three men in raincoats waited at the edge of the platform. Others were staked out around the ride so that all avenues of escape were closed.

"I do not care. It is a matter of honor," the wounded man growled, wiping his streaming nose with a handkerchief. "It iss the girl ve want, no?"

Nick looked back at the Bad German. His grin was taunting, infuriatingly wide. Suddenly the wounded man's hand stabbed at his shoulder looking for his gun. The

Good German struggled with him for a moment, then they were both half standing as the Bad German tried to pull away from his comrade's restraining grasp. He was half-balanced on the edge of the gondola when Nick stepped in.

Half rising and turning in his seat, Nick drove a karate chop to the back of the Bad German's neck and, as the man sagged back toward his seat, Nick's hand flashed out and caught him by the belt and propelled him out into empty space.

Nick saw him spinning against the trees and then the ride swept them away. A strange noise went up from the crowd below that sounded like a half sigh, surf in the rising wind, and then the machine was slowing, descending.

The machine came around full circle and Nick saw the inert body below him of the Bad German who was now also a Good German. The Good German who was still alive stared calmly at Nick with expressionless eyes.

"That was extremely foolhardy, Herr von Runstadt. While I do not wish to draw attention to our little transaction, be sure I will have no objection to shooting you if it becomes necessary," he said. "You will walk quietly out with us past the gate."

"Sure," Nick said.

Then he jumped out of the gondola. He hoped he'd judged the distance correctly. The ground seemed to be racing in two directions at once, then he hit with a thump that knocked the breath out of his lungs. His brain threatened to go black on him but somehow he forced himself to remain conscious. He staggered to his feet, his eyes clearing, and stabbed at his shoulder where the Luger was. Then the Luger was in his hand and he was firing almost without taking conscious aim. Two of the three black-coated figures on the platform fell and the other dived for protection.

People began yelling and running in all directions. Nick spun and found the gondola he had just jumped from. It hung where the ride man had automatically stopped it, as they did when they feared an accident, swaying about ten feet above the loading platform, and the Good German was staggering around inside the bucket trying to find his balance to shoot at him.

Nick braced himself and poured a full clip into the back of the gondola and saw the bullets cut through the thin sheet metal of the sides like the marks of a gigantic ice pick.

"Astrid . . . " Nick bellowed. The girl came to her feet, looking wildly around. Nick saw an arm come over the back seat and yank at her raincoat and he fired the Luger again and again. Then he saw the arm go limp.

He didn't even have to tell her what to do. Before she heard him yell she had tossed her high heels over the side of the gondola. A moment later she was hanging from the side by both hands. Nick had an instant's glimpse of delectable thighs revealed by the blowing skirt. Then she dropped like a sack of potatoes to the soggy turf. Nick dashed toward the heap of her raincoat and pulled the girl to her feet.

In the distance Nick could hear the whoop-whoop of European police sirens approaching. Leading the girl he ran once more for the concealing darkness, helping her over the fence around the ride.

They followed the winding walks of the park toward a special gate for performers in the outdoor ballet theater. This gate was not open to the public and perhaps von Stadee's men didn't have it covered.

They raced down the empty rows of dripping seats toward the tent-stage. The performance was long since over and the stage was empty of people, yet still set as an enchanted castle. Their footsteps resounded forlornly across the bare boards as Nick headed for the blackness of the backstage area.

Then an overhead spotlight flicked on. Nick shot it out with one sweeping movement. The light hissed out and the stage faded back into darkness.

The eerie laughter of the dwarf began again. Astrid moaned and clutched at Nick's arm. Then she slowly fell to the stage with a heavy thump. Nick cursed and dragged her behind a movable flat and tried to bring her around. When the long lashes parted and her eyes opened, those great green orbs stared back at him without recognition.

"Who are you—?" she faltered.

Nick struck her sharply. He had seen this happen before. Courage was something you had to keep in training for. And she belonged to another world. She wanted out, it was as simple as that.

"It's almost over, baby," he said softly. "You're home free."

"You're lying," she said. Her voice was strange and held a note of childish cunning. "I can still hear that laughing. It's monstrous . . ."

Nick struck her again.

"Knock it off, Astrid. It's me, Nick. Pull yourself together for just a little while longer. Then we really will be out of here."

Slowly the limp body of the girl became alert. She sat up and brushed her cascade of white-blonde hair back from her face.

"I am sorry. That was most unlike me."

"Wait," Nick whispered. Stealthily as death he began to mount the backstage ladder that led to the complex of lights above the stage. The Luger was in its holster again, for guns would bring the Count's men or the police, almost equally bad choices. Up the ladder he went, silent as only Killmaster could be. Soon his two hundred pounds was prowling the catwalk high above the stage listening for the sounds of breathing in the tangle of wires, ropes and pipes that littered the ceiling.

In the darkness a board creaked. A tiny breath rasped and the beginnings of a chuckle were sharply repressed. Nick advanced ten feet along the catwalk.

Then the whole stage burst into light as if the whole corps de ballet were about to come trooping out for a new performance. Nick was blinded by the lights. He stood defenseless and swaying on a thin plank seventy feet above the stage waiting for the dwarf's bullet.

Then the laughter started and like a man released from bondage Nick galvanized into action.

The dwarf stood fifteen feet away on the other end of the plank, his gnarled little face twisted into a hideous grimace. His knife flashed through the air like a silver bird and only Nick's magnificent reflexes saved him to meet his death at a later day. Nick hurled himself flat on the plank, throwing Hugo, his own beautifully balanced stiletto, from the shoulder as he fell.

The dwarf leaped into space as Nick's stiletto drove high into his shoulder blade. Nick heard the little man's howl of anguish and waited for it to be cut short by the impact of his fall. But the crash never came. Leaping to his feet, Nick saw the dwarf, his powerful arms and lightweight body catching hold of a supporting pipe as he fell, dropping with the agility of a monkey onto the next pipe and then scurrying up a ladder into the stygian darkness of the roof.

Nick attempted to follow but the little man was too swift and had the advantage of being almost weightless. He moved with the lithe speed of a retreating chimpanzee, an expert gymnast, and Nick with his size was no match for him at this monkey's game.

The heat of the lights reminded Nick that someone would arrive soon to find out why the lights were on in an empty theatre. The wounded dwarf's laughter died away in the darkness of the roof and Nick began his climb down to the stage.

He knew that one day he would silence that laughter forever but for now the little obscenity had won. Nick's job was to get Astrid Lundgren back to the Swedish Security Police.

He led her down the backstage area, past quiet dressing rooms to the stage door. They were out through an alley onto the wide Vesterborgade.

Car tires hissed by on the rain-wet streets, then Nick heard what he had been listening for, the swift clip-clop of horses' hooves and the sound of carriage wheels creaking against their axles. He looked up and down the street. No black raincoats. Not yet. They would be around somewhere but the Count hadn't been receiving signals from the transistorized receiver in Astrid's pocket and the Swedes had. Nick had a few minutes then.

With infuriating sedateness the horsedrawn beer cart approached the mouth of the alley. There it slowed but did not stop. The familiar mutton-chop whiskers of Vice Admiral Larson peered out from beneath the canvas that usually protected beer cases but tonight protected seven armed men and the head of Swedish Security.

"Had us just the littlest bit worried when you didn't come out, Mr. Carter. How's Madame Curie?"

"We went for a little row on the lake," Nick said cryptically, "and we all feel better now. If you'll just sign for the package I'll be on my way."

The girl and the head of Security changed places and the cart drew off, the driver puffing phlegmatically on his pipe as if he were hauling another load of beer instead of taking one of the most important scientists in the free world to a secluded airbase. There a flight by a Swedish Air Force plane would take her back to her futuristic underground lab in Sweden.

Nick stood in the dripping alley and drew with immense satisfaction on his first cigarette in hours. The craggy-faced Swede jammed his hands in his pocket.

"Von Stadee will have men here any minute," Nick said. "Where can we talk?"

"Ny Havn."

Ny Havn was a narrow street along a dark tree-lined canal. The cellars and ground floors of the houses were given over to a series of fly-by-night jazz clubs and from the open doors jukeboxes blared and the wail of saxophones filtered up to the street. Even on this dismal night the clubs were crowded with tow-headed, dungareed youth gyrating on the postage stamp dance floors. Even if Count von Stadee, who sometimes seemed to be everywhere, had foreseen their rendezvous, the six Danish sidemen working on "That Old Time Religion" would have made the most sophisticated of listening devices useless.

Nick drank his Carlsberg in two long pulls, coming down to earth after the tension of action.

"On the whole," he said, "it worked pretty well. The Count and I have what is called an involvement. Holding your men back was a good idea. He still thinks I'm a free lance with perhaps a small gang."

"When I saw those Danish police go into the park, I began to grow a white hair for each second that passed," the Security man said.

"It was worth it," Nick grinned. "By tomorrow I'll have my foot in the door. But I'll need help. I don't know this country very well. And the Count is big. Just how big I don't know yet."

Nick outlined his idea and the bearded Security chief nodded and made notes. A half hour later they left separately. Nick pulled the collar of his coat around him and strolled back to his hotel along the canal. As he stared at its slow, murky waters, he reflected that if he made the slightest misplay of his hand, by tomorrow night his body might be part of the refuse bobbing in the cold, dirty water.

Even the fact that it was all for the safety of America did not make the idea any more cheering.

CHAPTER 7

THE HELGOLAND ROAD ran for long stretches over flat farmland and rolling, fir-clad hills. The fat lowering clouds seemed to almost touch the thatched farm houses and the grayness of the day cast the road and the countryside into a monochromatic dullness.

The man in the old Jaguar sat parked in front of a small roadside restaurant and waited patiently. Then a speck appeared far up the road and grew quickly larger. Then it became a big BMW motorcycle which flashed in front of the restaurant doing better than a hundred miles an hour and still picking up speed. The rider in black leathers and crash helmet bent like a jockey over the handlebars, coaxing every inch of speed out of the great machine.

A slight smile spread across the face of the man at the wheel of the Jag.

"You're late, Boots," he said softly to himself. Quickly he pulled a knitted wool skier's mask over his head. The colored embellishment around the nose, eyes and mouth of the mask gave him a fierce mystic appearance of an ancient Aztec priest. When the mask was securely in place he pulled the sports car away from the restaurant and sped after the motorcycle.

At this point the motorcyclist was unaware of the pursuer. The flat stretch of road was almost ended and the needle of the speedometer hovered around 120 mph. Reluctantly, the rider throttled down and straightened up in the saddle. At that speed a hay truck or a farm horse in the road would be fatal. Even a patch of cow dung. A slight smile appeared on the wind-torn lips of the rider. This was a crummy butter and eggs country but with a

70

little luck Ricky, the Count, would have finished up his business in a few days and they could split. She, Boots Delaney, remembered the days when she had led up to a hundred outlaw bikes in a roaring hell-for-leather pack through the small towns of Southern California and Nevada and had the local fuzz so terrorized that they damn near called the National Guard every time the gang stopped to tap a kidney or something. And here she was worrying about cowflops on the road for God's sake.

The thought of her boyfriend Ricky or Count Ulrich von Stadee, sent a queer thrill through her slim youthful body. Boots had seen plenty of guys whom their own mothers would have described as hard cases but Ricky was the hardest, toughest and, incidentally, the most successful outlaw she had ever met. Or heard of, for God's sake. He operated almost always inside the law and the number of rackets he was in was fantastic. To say nothing of the Knights—that small army of military-type studs who yelled out "how much" the second Ricky said "spit."

The great motorcycle throbbed and roared between her thighs and Boots sat there feeling tingly as she thought about her man and his lean hard body. She spotted the sports car a couple of miles behind her but paid no attention to it because her thoughts were in that strange room in the castle. Ricky was hard as a rock because he trained like a prizefighter and Boots yearned for the touch of that masculine form dominating her own slim suppleness. But in seven months Ricky hadn't touched her as man to woman. "Women weaken men's will," he said in that strange voice. "The key is discipline. To lead you must be able to bear more than others." It was then when poor Boots was aching and burning with unrequited passion that Ricky forced her to apply herself to his body with the whips and thongs and heated irons that decorated the master bedroom. As a demonstration of courage, Boots thought it was impressive. It certainly scared her and she was no softie, but as a substitute for the old slap and tickle it was definitely unsatisfactory.

And, of late, she had noticed that Ricky seemed to be getting a little more out of their nightly sessions than discipline—to her wise young eyes it looked damned close to fun he was having—and she was gaining a strange power over him. Although Boots was a child of the gutter, she was astute enough to know that power could turn against its possessor . . .

She didn't get a chance to finish the thought. The slob in the Jag was right behind her, blasting away on his horn. There was plenty of room to pass so Boots made a gesture with an upraised arm that is a recognized insult from pole to pole.

The sports car drifted out beside her and edged in tight. Boots looked over at the driver to hurl another insult and damned near laid the bike down right there. This weird kind of birdman in the car was pointing her, Boots, over to the side of the road like some kind of science-fiction traffic cop.

"Like hell, buddy," Boots screamed. She twisted the throttle on the BMW to full and the motorcycle leaped forward like a spirited horse. Boots crouched low over the handlebars while the wind whipped at her face. Farm houses, woods and meadows flashed by in a continuous blur as the needle of her speedometer kept on climbing.

Already her shrewd young brain was examining the situation carefully. The Count was involved in big things. Like any powerful man he had rivals. And Boots was the Count's recognized mistress. Through her the rivals could put pressure on the Count. Von Stadee could be very unpleasant about mistakes, and Boots had a pretty shrewd idea that he would consider her letting herself be captured as a serious blunder.

She checked the rear-view mirror. The sports car was coming up fast. The man in the mask seemed to know what to do behind the wheel. He went through a bend in the road with all the skill of a Grand Prix driver and kept gaining on her.

Swiftly the girl reviewed the topography of the surrounding country. She had ridden along this road often. She recognized three houses at the top of a knoll. It seemed to her that there was a watering pool for cattle and a dirt road that ran off into the woods, a curve just ahead of it to conceal her action. She went through the curve using an old trick that the county circuit riders used to get around corners at high speed. The bike struck sparks on the road and canted dangerously over, then suddenly she was through. A minute later she was jouncing up the rough dirt at reduced speed making for the safety of the woods.

The man in the Jag should be powering past like a bat out of hell and she would be far into the deep boondocks by the time he realized that she was off the road. A feeling of relief and triumph surged through her. Ricky would have been nasty about her letting herself get snatched by some sort of Danish hood.

The roar of the Jaguar's motor magnified behind her. She turned to watch it go by. Then with a shock of horror she realized that the masked man hadn't been fooled. The Jag raced into sight around the curve and practically without cutting its speed swept smoothly into the dirt road and came jouncing up the slope after her.

Boots prepared to give it one last try on the bike and then she saw the gate, a barrier of firm pine logs blocking her path. She realized her mistake. On the open road she had had a chance. Someone might have seen her and called the cops, but up in these quiet woods the masked man had her all to himself. As the throbbing of the BMW engine died, she realized how very much alone she was. The only sound in the trees was the whisper of wind and the flutter of a passing bird. Desperately, knowing that she was trapped, she began to run.

Behind her the Jag growled to a halt. She heard a car door slam loudly in the stillness of the wood. Then she saw the masked man running swiftly and easily through the trees. Down the slope was an open meadow and across the wet meadow lay a farm house. Boots made for the meadow at top speed, cursing the heavy motorcycle boots that sunk into the damp earth at every step and seemed to anchor her to the ground. At least maybe in the meadow someone would see her. Where *were* the cops in this damned country?

She splashed through the wet fields toward the rick of fodder where sleepy cows stood up to their ankles in the spring grass and nibbled. The man's footsteps squished heavily on behind her. Then Boots had an inspiration. She stumbled heavily and lay face down in the water while the man approached. Under the concealment of her body she drew the long-bladed knife that rode in the inset of her left boot.

As the man came up on her Boots sprang to her feet like a scalded cat, her beautiful young face twisted with rage, the knife lashing out furiously at the masked man's belly.

"Come and get it, big stud," the girl snarled. "Anything you can take, you can keep."

The masked man drifted away from the deadly blade as gracefully as a dancer and circled her steadily. Boots' deadly little rushes only brought a pleasant chuckle from him.

"Give it up, Boots. I'm not a Southern California deputy."

Boots' reply was an unprintable burst of profanity. Then the masked man made his move with the speed of a striking rattlesnake. He came in under her weapon, caught her knife hand and exerted a quick pressure on a certain part of her wrist. The knife went sailing away into the hayrick. In another moment he had produced a chloroformed rag and held it firmly over her face against her wildest struggles. The girl's clear blue eyes were twin pinpoints of hate as she fought against her captor's grip but he was as strong as iron and his eyes seemed to smile gently at her struggles through the slits in his mask.

His eyes seemed to swim in front of her. She tried to think of some other threat to make and then the scene went black.

She was lying on a bed, a big comfortable bed, and she was in a house. That much she could be sure of. It was an odd sort of a house because the windows were boarded up solidly and the roof where it touched the walls was made of something that looked like straw. She decided that it must be one of those farm houses that she had passed so often. Well, at least she seemed to still be in Denmark.

Across the room a large man squatted with his back to her, getting a fire going in the great stone fireplace that occupied half of one wall. From his size and the catlike efficiency of his movements, Boots guessed it was the masked man out of uniform. But her hands were free and she wasn't going to wait around to find out for sure.

With the quickness of youth she was off the bed and sprinting for the door. The man looked over his shoulder with an ironic smile. Boots hit the door at full speed and attempted to tear it open. It was locked of course. With a scream of rage she flung herself at that smiling face, scratching, kicking and sobbing curses. Without apparently discomoding himself in the slightest, the big man scooped her up in his arms and tossed her halfway across the room where she bounced like a trampoline artist on the big fourposter bed.

The man waited patiently while she ran out of curses and breath at about the same time and lay staring at him with the angry eyes of a cat that has fallen into the bathtub.

"Where are we and what are we doing here?" she asked weakly. Even as her rage subsided her curiosity was getting the better of her. Her young-old eyes noted the way the expensive shirt stretched across his powerful chest, the strength in the good looking, yet hard face and the humor in the deep-set gray eyes.

"We're waiting for the Count," the big man said. He spoke with the trace of a British accent that was common to educated Germans who had learned their English before 1939. "Your boyfriend has a truly remarkable organization. It took all afternoon for me to get you here. I thought there's nothing like a cozy fire to take the chill off these cold spring evenings."

"I know you," Boots said. "You're that German soldier of fortune Ricky was talking with at the ballet. Von Runstadt."

The man nodded and went back to poking the fire. Boots curled up on the bed catlike.

"Ricky will kill you, baby," she said silkily. Nick Carter laughed.

"He's already tried that. What's worse he tried to steal something from me. Now I've stolen something from him."

"That's not the way the game is played, mister," she said. She was irritated and half attracted by the big man's casual dismissal of von Stadee's power. "That man is more powerful than the Chancellor of Germany. You just don't steal things from him, especially his chick."

"Isn't that interesting?" Nick said. He tried a shrewd guess. "I wouldn't have put your friend Rick down as a guy who was interested in chicks. Not primarily, anyway."

The girl flushed and Nick knew that he had come close to the mark.

"Ricky is a great man," she said heatedly.

"And I'll bet he'd tell me so himself if he were here," Nick grinned.

"You'll find out when he gets you back to Germany. Ever hear of the Teutonic Knights?"

"Seems to me I have. In fact I'll tell you a secret," Nick said. "That's why I put the snatch on you, Boots. Von Stadee loused up my only chance for a little pin money so now I have to find a job. You're my only application to the Teutonic Knights. I won't get his answer until tomorrow morning so we might as well make ourselves comfortable."

"You'll be dead tomorrow morning," the girl said with conviction.

"One of these mornings we'll all be dead, kid," Nick said, "but let's not lose any sleep. By the way, before I can turn my back on you with any confidence, I'll have to ask you to get out of those leathers long enough for me to find out if you have any more of those pig stickers on you. There's a shirt over there you can put on."

Boot's alert young face grew sultry with anger. She stiffened on the bed and her eyes narrowed.

"Don't get funny with me, mister. When Ricky gets you, I can make the way you go out easy or hard."

Nick stuck a cigarette in his mouth and eyed her steadily. Although he had already frisked her for a gun she could be concealing anything up to a harpoon under those leathers.

"The clothes, Boots. I wish I were a gentleman, but I'm not."

"Mister, you can . . ."

"Nobody loves a garbage mouth, Boots," Nick said gently. "Out of the leathers and into the shirt."

Sulkily the girl rolled over on her back and lay staring at the ceiling.

"Come and take them off yourself, lover man. And remember that for every finger you lay on me Ricky will have you spend a week in his experimental ward at the hospital."

Reluctantly Nick rose and approached the supine girl. In a second she was off the bed, a switchblade gleaming in her fist. Nick laughed and sidestepped her first vicious thrust and knocked the blade out of her hand with a casual blow that left her hand hanging numbly at her side. Good God, Nick wondered, how many more of those things did she have concealed on her? Those damned leather suits had more tricks than a performing seal. Already she was trying to get at one of the innumerable zipper pockets in the jacket with her good hand. Nick caught her by the lapels of the jacket and lifted her off the floor with one hand. Then he shook her until she stopped trying to get at the pocket and dropped her on the bed. She was all driving knees and clawing hands until Nick laid one big hand gently but firmly over her face, shutting off her air supply. With his free hand he unzipped the jacket and worked her out of it. It took a behind toehold to get the boots off. Then he put one foot in the middle of her back and pulled the leggings off by the ankles. With the pile of clothes he walked over to the couch and sat down.

Boots sat on the bed clad only in bra and panties and watched him with smoldering eyes, her sharp Irish face tense with hate and her slim body quivering with rage

An inside zipper pocket turned up a pair of brass knuckles and a patch pocket on the leggings revealed a straight razor.

"I know you've got a hand grenade around here somewhere," Nick laughed, "but since I can't find it you might as well keep it."

Boots said nothing but her small white breasts heaved expressively. Nick tossed her the shirt.

"I don't want your damned shirt, mister," Boots snarled.

"All right take the security and happiness jacket."

She put the leather jacket back on, propped herself against the head of the bed, her long slim legs stretched out in front of her, and puffed angrily away at a cigarette while Nick brought out sandwiches, fruit and cold Danish beer. After a couple of refusals for form's sake, Boots allowed herself to be persuaded to join Nick, who was wolfing the sandwiches and washing them down with long swallows of beer with the air of a man who has put in an honest day's kidnaping.

"What did you tell the Count you were going to do with me if he didn't meet your demands?" she asked.

"I said if the ransom money wasn't promptly paid, I'd do my worst and send you to do some post-graduate work at a good New England girls' finishing school," Nick laughed.

"We'll see how hard you laugh when Ricky gets through with you," the girl said sourly. Nick looked at his watch. He was getting just a little tired of hearing about the incomparable Count von Stadee. It was late and he had a lot to do tomorrow. He arranged a blanket on the couch and turned off the lights. By the light of the fire he saw the supple-bodied girl walk with her leggy stride toward the bed. Her hair was down around her shoulders and the big jacket made her look small and frail. The fire was warm against his flesh as he stripped and stretched in front of the couch.

"Herr von Runstadt? Nick?" the girl said softly. She came toward him on bare feet. "Maybe I've got you wrong. I'm not much good at saying I'm sorry . . ."

Somewhere along the line she had slipped out of her bra and panties and now only the black leather jacket protected her vulnerable young flesh. The flickering firelight laved the long white thighs and cast highlights on the small soft breasts. Nick felt the heat of the fire along the corded muscles of his thighs and lower belly mingling with the stirring of a different kind of heat. She came around the couch, disregarding the fact that he was stark naked and extended a slim hand. Her Irish blue eyes were glinting with warmth and humor.

"Why should we be enemies?"

Nick raised a quizzical eyebrow. Then before he could stop her, the girl darted to the fireplace and seized the poker which had been lying in the flames all afternoon and turned on him with a cry of triumph. Damn, Nick thought, careless of me. She's had her eye on that since supper. The glowing red tip of the poker feinted at his head and then flashed in at his groin. Nick leaped backwards, feeling its searing heat, and fell on the couch. The girl thrust again laughing triumphantly and Nick rolled desperately along the couch staying just out of reach of the red hot iron.

"How do you like it, mister?" the girl said. Her small white teeth flashed in a bitchy little grin. "Come take this away, tiger. You can get a knife to make things even."

Nick was rolling across the floor, trying to get to his feet.

"Damned sporting of you, kid," he managed to mutter. He got the table between himself and the lunging girl and circled while she thrust the heated poker across at him like a rapier of fire. Perhaps he could lure her away from the fire.

"You're going to get tired of running, mister," Boots said.

"Don't you believe it, kid," Nick said. "Anyway, in a minute I'm going to take that away from you and I may not have the time to be gentle. Stop wasting our time."

"You're going to let me out of here in five minutes or get the poker right up the old you know where."

"You're right, Boots," Nick laughed. "I can't see you in finishing school."

He walked out from behind the table and stood balanced lightly on the balls of his feet, over two hundred pounds of athletic manhood poised to move like a cat in any direction. For the first time Nick saw the girl falter. Then she looked at the hot iron in her hand and her courage returned.

"Give us back the poker," Nick said softly. "I mean it, kid."

Boots' eyes gleamed with a strange brightness. She began to giggle softly as Nick tensed himself for the attack. Her gaze roamed the long hard muscles of Nick's body. She began to retreat slowly and just as slowly Nick advanced on her. The thrill of the stalk began to rise in Nick. His little head feints were making her nervous. She knew now from experience how fast Nick could move when he wanted to.

She retreated around the couch, her lithe body trembling with excitement. The poker described fiery little circles in the air and suddenly Nick was aware that the hunt had changed into something more subtle and exciting. The hot iron was the barrier that must be conquered before the maiden would give herself. If he disarmed her then her German superman would at least be temporarily forgotten in the thrill of the hunted woman, but if she burned him badly or laid his head open then von Stadee would reign supreme.

Nick grinned at her. To her surprise she grinned back freely and openly, a nice Irish smile.

"Come on," she said softly, from deep in her throat. It was half a woman's invitation and half a bitch's challenge. She too was poised, her slender white legs ready to move in any direction. With one hand she pulled the jacket wide exposing the slim soft belly and lovely little breasts. Her body, white as skimmed milk, welcomed him but, on the other hand, the glowing poker hissed its challenge in the air.

Suddenly Nick was a tawny flash of rippling muscle streaking in under the iron barrier of the poker. Her slender arm flashed with the quick viciousness of a rider beating a horse as the red hot poker cut wickedly at Nick's head. She missed and tried to dance away but Nick blocked the second blow. As she stumbled backward, trying to get in a third, he knocked it out of her hand to the floor and fell with her in a tangle of limbs to the bed. She tried to free herself to reach the poker on the floor but Nick caught her with one powerful arm and held her firmly on the bed. For a moment she continued to struggle with a surprisingly wiry strength. Then she was laughing a deep rich laugh, still struggling but not to get away. Her body was cool and her sharp white teeth were attacking his body at a dozen points, sending bright messages of desire into his brain.

Somewhere along the way the leather jacket came off. There were few preliminaries.

The buildup had been too intense and the wait too long. His hands were running up and down her exposed young back, then cupping the small hard breasts with an uninhibited mixture of violence and tenderness. She moved beneath him like a young wild thing and suddenly her long legs were apart and her thin hands were strong on his back driving him to her. She moaned once long and low at the hot sweetness of their meeting.

After that there was only wildness, speed and more speed which seemed to be drawn out endlessly. She attacked on all sides, in every position and when his strength sought to force her down she wriggled free and offered her body in another position.

"My God, so long . . ." she whispered at one point. Then suddenly with a great shuddering the two taut bodies were drained of the burning silver of the moment and they slowly subsided. She lay stretched out in his arms, running her fingers through the dampness of his hair.

They lay in silence in the dark until by the slow movement of her body and her questing, caressing hands she indicated the rebirth of her desire. The second passing was more deliberate, more of a display of virtuosity on both their parts but no less rewarding. With it came a companionable intimacy. The girl lay on her back and talked at random, telling stories of the motorcycle gangs of California, the Grand Prix racing circuit, her meeting with von Stadee at the Nürburgring race and her time as his mistress. Nick's voice was casual and lazy as he prompted her with a joke or a question but he was once more the professional, disguising a pointed question with a joke.

Late in the evening she broke the lengthening silence. "I still owe you something for making me look like a fool and Boots Delaney always pays her debts," she said sleepily. "But I guess I can take my time paying you off."

In the dark Nick chuckled softly.

CHAPTER 8

THE TORCHLIGHTS cast flickering shadows on the massive stones of the old German castle. The cobbled square was filled with a seething mass of good-natured masculine faces and a thousand voices were bellowing, laughing and screaming odds. Nick turned his sweating face into the cool breeze blowing off the barge canal. Boots had been wrong about von Stadee killing Nick. Instead he had given Nick a job. Nick hadn't left him much choice. No job, no Boots. Right now, though, Nick almost wished von Stadee had refused. The Teutonic Knights had a strange enlistment procedure.

A roar went up from the crowd and interrupted his thoughts. Nick drew a weary breath. The other guy, the Great Gildersleeve or whoever the hell he was, was entering the ring. Nick's handlers, two smiling German jocks, kneaded the muscles in Nick's shoulders.

"One last effort, Herr von Runstadt," one of the handlers enthused, clapping Nick on the shoulder. "You have only to stay one round and you will have the second highest score ever achieved."

Nick took a look at the opposition. He was a mountain of a man, solid as the Great Pyramid, with coal-black burning eyes and a black sergeant-major's moustache. Heinrich, that was the name. Nick remembered hearing that he had been European Professional Wrestling Champion until he had killed a man in the ring and maimed several others. Finally he had been stripped of his title but from the way they were cheering him, the Teutonic Knights seemed to think he was just fine. Unenthusiastically, Nick watched Heinrich strut around the ring joking with the spectators.

Count von Stadee approached Nick's corner.

"Permit me to congratulate you, Herr von Runstadt."
Von Stadee was accompanied by his usual entourage of
officers of the Teutonic Knights and Boots, looking very
cool and feminine in a tailored dress that fitted her slim
lines the way sails fitted a clipper ship. "Your performance today has been most impressive. Childish, you
may think these feats of strength and skill, but was it not
Wellington who said it was upon the playing fields of Eton
that the Battle of Waterloo was won? At any rate our
younger auxiliaries derive great enjoyment from the spec-
tacle even if, perhaps for our professional officers, the
games become a bit tiresome. But you have really com-
piled a remarkable record." The Count cocked his head
and regarded Nick with narrowed eyes. "Of course such
might have been expected from a man of your audacity
and ingenuity."

"*Danke*," Nick said. "Thanks." Taciturnity, he decided,
might also have been expected from him at this point. He
felt as if he had just finished competing in the Olympic
Decathlon. Since dawn he had been running, shooting,
taking tests and doing all the other things that a potential
officer in a new super-elite corps might be expected to
excel at. Now there was only this last hand-to-hand combat event. When it was over he would have finished the
Test of Excellence and become one of the boys, a neo-
Nazi in good standing.

"I wish you the best of luck in your endeavors against
the good Heinrich," von Stadee said suavely. "Let me
caution you that he grows a bit vicious when pressed too
hard. His last combat was against a particularly promising
candidate, an exceptional specimen who stayed for six
rounds. Unfortunately the fellow was of little use to us
with a broken spine. Since, however, you need only one
round to compile a score second only to my own, I would
advise you to stay out of his reach and more or less resign
early in the second round. I barely managed three myself

and would have been perhaps wiser if I had bowed gracefully to the inevitable at the end of the second."

Laughter went up from the officers around von Stadee
and Nick realized the Count had made a joke. The joke
had a point. The point was that von Stadee didn't want
Nick beating his record. From the way Nick felt right now
there was little danger of that. Then a bell rang and
Horrible Heinrich was advancing across the ring. Nick's
handlers gave him a shove and he realized that the fight
was on. There was no referee for the plain and simple
reason that there were no rules. Anything went. Nick
cursed his weary limbs into action and circled warily.
Somewhere a beer keg hissed and the crowd moaned with
anticipation. The mountainous German was coming on
like a wrestler with his hands down low and his weight
well distributed for a move in any direction. Nick promptly flashed in and slammed a right into the giant's jaw that
sent daggers of pain up to his shoulder blade. The giant
grunted, shook off the blow and seized Nick around the
waist with an arm like a shoulder of beef. Then he drove
his massive knee up into Nick's crotch. A sigh of disappointment spread through the crowd. They feared an early
K.O. and an end to this sport, but at the last possible
second Nick twisted around and avoided the pile-driving
knee. At the same time he drove the base of his hand
against the mass of scar tissue that was Heinrich's nose.
The giant grunted and drew in a breath through his mouth
but otherwise showed no ill effects. Nick snapped a karate
blow to the windpipe which should have broken it or at
least bent it badly. Heinrich coughed and grunted.

Nick danced away and drummed a tattoo of blows to
the giant's body that had the crowd on its feet cheering
wildly but Heinrich wasn't even staggered. God, was the
monster human? That last combination had contained
some of Nick's best stuff and here was old Heinrich
moving around fresh as a daisy, his gorilla-like arms
pawing ahead of him like the tentacles of an octopus. Nick
closed for a little judo. That had to work, he reasoned.

Tough as Heinrich seemed to be, he was subject to certain mechanical laws like the rest of the world.

Perhaps it was because Nick was close to exhaustion and the German was fresh. Perhaps it was because Nick's timing was a hair's breadth off. Suddenly he found himself lifted from the ground and flying through the air. The ring rope passed beneath him and there was a scrambling in the crowd. Then he came down heavily on a cushion of beer-filled bellies.

Hoarse masculine voices cursed roundly in German. Someone spilled a beer. Its cooling foam cascaded down Nick's forehead bringing him back to reality. Heinrich was strutting around the ring, gesturing to the crowd and clasping his hands overhead. Nick shook his head groggily. His overwhelming impulse was to lie where he was. He had already passed the tests; he was in. Suddenly hands lifted him up and shoved him back toward the ring. More hands reached out for him and like some unwilling centipede Nick was propelled back toward stage center. Three burly Teutons gave him a last assist into the ring and Nick found himself staggering in a daze toward Heinrich the Gigantic German. Oh well, Jack Dempsey had once come back in the same way to win.

"Ach, the *wunderkind* is back for more," Heinrich grunted. Nick shook his head to clear the daze. It was good to know the fellow could talk, anyway, he thought. At least it proved they belonged to the same species.

"That's right, fatso," Nick said. He licked blood from his lips and grinned. "We're going to flatten you, big boy, and get some cadets to shave off that ugly mustache."

The German growled something guttural and obscene and fired a savage kick at Nick's head. Nick caught the blow on his shoulder but it still hit him like the kick of a mule and he dropped to the canvas. Heinrich leaped high in the air and came down knees first on Nick's back. His breath was expelled in a rush leaving him gagging and choking. His eyes saw only a dark haze, his lungs felt ringed with fire. He realized slowly that the German was knocking his head against the floor.

The darkness came and went with every blow. It occurred to Nick that all his infiltration of the Teutonic Knights would do little good if he died during the qualifying tests. He heard his handlers shouting from the corner to hang on, there was only one minute left in the round. Good Lord, had all this taken only two minutes? Nick felt as if he'd been in combat for months on end. He drew on the last reserves of his energy to gather himself together. The German was getting careless now, varying his holds to please the crowd.

Nick came to life as tricky and vicious as a boated shark, driving his foot into the man's face with all the explosive strength of his powerful thigh behind the blow. Heinrich reeled back with a surprised look on his animal face. Nick came to his feet like a cat and hurled himself feet first through the air at Heinrich's head. Again Nick's weight exploded in the big German's face. Both men slapped the mat together but Nick got up again and the German lay twitching on his back gasping for air. Slowly he began to climb to his feet but halfway up he changed his mind and lashed out at Nick's groin with one boulder-like fist. Nick dodged away and caught him by his wide ears, then he slammed his knee repeatedly into the giant's face. Unexpectedly the giant let out a bellow of pain, some subhuman cry of anguish that issued from the bloody, pulpy face like the death agony of a dinosaur. Nick let him drop.

A silence fell over the crowd. They had not expected this. Heinrich tottered weakly to his feet and staggered forward. Nick's face was a pitiless warrior's mask. It was he who was working on the last resources of his strength not Horrible Heinrich. Give the monster the period between rounds to recover and he would eat Nick alive in the second round, perhaps kill him for the humiliation of the first round.

Nick snapped off another series of combinations and,

when the giant still failed to hit the deck, Nick caught him in a headlock and then ran with him to the ring post at full speed, driving Heinrich's bullet head into the iron post with their combined weight behind it. Seeing what Nick was up to, the crowd came to its feet, the blood lust high and keening as with one voice, the Teutonic Knights began to chant out the time as Nick smashed the great ugly head with a steady rhythm. In the corner Nick's handlers bellowed and slapped each other joyfully on the back. And slowly, finally, the giant's legs gave way beneath him. Nick was no longer strong enough to hold him up. With a last karate chop to the back of the neck, Nick let Heinrich drop to the ring mat where he lay as still as a stone, and the massed students and officers filled the night with pandemonium.

The cheering went on and on. The handlers were in the ring joyfully toweling Nick's back. Someone handed him a stein of beer. Nick let the cold fluid slide down his parched throat and held onto the ring ropes for support with his other hand.

"You have surpassed even Count von Stadee. No man has previously defeated Heinrich and no man has achieved a higher score on the Test of Excellence."

The handlers babbled about running Nick for Chancellor of Germany while the hero himself hung glassy eyed on the ring ropes. Somehow his eyes found the Count's party. Boots, he noted, was screaming with the rest, bless her little criminal heart, but the look on the Count's face made his blood run cold. "Beware, my lord, of jealousy." Those burning poet's eyes were fixed on Nick as if they were rivets that would sear his guts forever.

Then suddenly von Stadee was in the ring screaming for silence. His booted foot dispersed a good-natured crew of collegians who were attempting to cut off Heinrich's mustache with their Swiss Army Officer's knives.

Von Stadee's voice grew high and shrill as he screamed at the riotous crowd.

"Silence, you contemptible curs. You are not German

youth but beer-drinking pigs ... not fighting wolves but whipped curs who have seen their master. A man has appeared who makes the cream of German youth look like children at play and yet you cheer. Is this how the indignities of the past will be avenged ... by such as you?"

Slowly the shouting died. The crowd noise grew to an embarrassed murmur. Then silence. Only the ranting voice of the Count echoed from the walls of the old university town. Nick hung on the ropes and listened. The Count went on for some minutes while white-coated doctors carried Heinrich from the ring and the crowd shuffled nervously and listened to its master.

Von Stadee read his young troopers the riot act for twenty minutes, barely pausing for breath, and finished by promising them double drills and reduced privileges. Then he left the ring, still trembling with rage, to be driven home. Once the Count's Mercedes had departed the mood again became celebratory. It was declared that Nick must have a triumph and presently they bore him away on their shoulders by torchlight so that he might enter the town by the Blucher Gate. As the noisy crowd filed along the canal, the torches made dancing lights on the dark water's surface and Nick reflected that the scene could as well have been Heidelberg in 1937. Jackboots echoed on the cobblestones. Hearty masculine voices sang of love and conquest. Presently they took him to the *Deutschland Uber Alles Tavern* and made much of him. Red-faced and sweating they came up to throw their hairy arms around him and call him comrade. Nick bore the nonsense as civilly as he could and kept sober by concentrating on the white-bosomed barmaids in peasant blouses. And somewhere over the course of the evening he saw a face that he recognized. It took him a moment to place it, then he had it. Sweden. The little crew-cut man with the popeyes who had locked him in the morgue with the blue body of the scientist. Only now he was serving beer to the army of red-faced crew-cut youth at the long trestle tables. Nick leaped to his feet.

"*Entschuldigen sie,* excuse me, comrades," Nick roared. "I go now to return the good beer of Bavaria to the good earth of Bavaria so that there may be room for more." He struggled free of the comradely arms about his shoulders, then he reversed his field and cut sharply in the direction of the little morgue attendant who was now a waiter. The waiter saw him coming and his popeyes widened with terror. In his confusion he dropped a tray of full beer steins in the lap of a gigantic leader of cadets and ran pell-mell for the door. Nick burst out the door ten steps behind him but fear lent speed to the little man's footsteps. Nick chased the little ghoul for two blocks and overhauled him with a burst of speed as the waiter cut across an arched stone bridge.

Nick caught him by his shirt and slammed him against the wall of the bridge. The man's teeth chattered.

"No . . . no . . . a mistake," the little man blurted.

"It sure was," Nick agreed.

"It was an accident. I swear."

"It was an accident that I lived, you mean." Nick's mind raced as he glared into the terror-filled eyes of the little waiter. If the man ever informed the Count that Nick had been moving around official Swedish circles all Nick's hard won infiltration would have been in vain. And the last chance of finding out who was really sabotaging Sweden's underground city and America's air defense would be lost. The stiletto appeared in Nick's hand.

The waiter's voice became shrill as the frightened words tumbled out.

"I didn't lock the door. I was as frightened then as I am now when you appeared out of the dark."

Nick placed the needle sharp point of the dagger against the man's trembling throat.

"Who killed the real morgue attendant?"

"I don't know."

"Wrong answer," Nick said. "It just cost you your life."

He clapped his hand over the man's mouth. The sad staring eyes widened and blinked rapidly as the man plucked at Nick's sleeve. Nick released his grip for a second.

"I'll bet you just remembered," Nick snarled.

"All right, I know, I know," the man said miserably. "One of von Stadee's lieutenants, Müller."

"Why?" Nick snapped. The man shrugged slowly and a measure of dignity returned.

"You will kill me but I don't know. This will probably cost me my life anyway."

"Then what the hell were you doing there?" Nick rasped. "Trying to sell the real attendant more insurance before your friends did him in?"

"My name is Gustav Lang. I am a reporter for *Der Spiegel* on special assignment. I'm doing a series on neo-Nazism in modern Germany and I've been keeping my eye on von Stadee for months now. You can check that with the editors if you have the contacts. If you don't, they won't tell you a thing."

Nick nodded. Checking that story wouldn't be difficult.

"I'd still like to know what happened to that morgue attendant."

The little man shook his head.

"When I heard von Stadee was up to something in Sweden, I went on up myself. I kept an eye on Müller and his other men in Sweden and talked with some newspaper contacts and began to learn about the emission rays that are hampering progress on their anti-laser experiments. When I heard about one of their top scientists dying I put two and two together and went to have a look. The morgue attendant was already dead so I hid him for awhile and had the opportunity to have a look around. I took his clothes because I'm very good at disguises. You may think that was a little cold-hearted but I've been around here long enough to know that von Stadee is up to a great deal more than leading songs around the campfires with his boy scouts here in Bavaria. I had to find out more. Then I ran into you ..." The little reporter shuddered at the memory. "I knew I had to get out of there fast."

There was a silence broken only by the lapping of the canal waters while Nick considered the story. Then he lit a cigarette and offered one to the reporter.

"I think you and I should have a long talk one of these days. But not now. I'd better get back to the party. Before I go there's one thing I'd like to know, Gus. Why is von Stadee interested in Sweden's defenses? Sweden was a neutral in the last war."

"Well," Gus said, "I can make only an educated guess but I hear things at the café. I'm pretty sure that it's this. When he pulls his coup against the government in Bonn, naturally NATO will withdraw all their atomic weapons faster than you can say *Mein Kampf*. But if von Stadee can keep Sweden from perfecting an anti-laser device, China will give him atomic weapons and a rudimentary delivery system as a reward. Then he'll rule Europe. And from the way scientists are turning blue and dying I'd say that he might hold a seat on the Board in America too. How do you like them *wiener schnitzels*?"

"I don't," Nick said. "When does all this happen?"

Gus shrugged.

"As soon as he can find an excuse. The next time the government is embarrassed. He's in with the industrialists and a great part of the military because of his father. They trust him but America and de Gaulle won't so he can't do anything big until he gets those Chinese A bombs. And the way international science is shying away from anti-laser experiments, that could be any day now."

"That's quite a story you've got, even for *Der Spiegel*," Nick said.

"I wish I could print one tenth of it," the little man said quietly. "Instead we'll hand Europe to a madman and America to China so that our publisher won't get sued."

Nick laughed without humor. There wasn't much point

in cabling Washington. If Hawk caught wind of this situation he'd just send in Nick Carter to look around. But Nick Carter was already there and without one good idea.

CHAPTER 9

NICK LAY SMOKING in a shaft of watery moonlight, his great shoulders and chest outside the covers. Through the casement windows he could see the castle grounds, pleasant enough by day, but now illuminated by the dim moon, menacing and hostile. If things went wrong there was no escape hatch from the Count's castle. At night killer dogs roamed the grounds in packs and, besides, the castle was so remote from any main thoroughfare that Nick would be hauled down in a couple of hours by patrols of those same cheerful young men with whom he had been singing and drinking two hours ago. In addition, the forest surrounding the castle was set with thousands of wolf traps which fired cyanide pellets, when tripped, like an exploding hand grenade.

At the same time, the possibility that von Stadee intended to use his enormous influence in Germany to unseat the Government in Bonn had to get to Washington even if it wasn't yet "hard information." Perhaps Gus himself would make a good courier, Nick thought. The little man seemed free to come and go as he pleased. There were difficulties there too but serious money usually overcame serious obstacles.

A draft of dank castle air blew across Nick's bare chest. From the outside these old castles looked like something on a travel poster but inside they were about as comfortable as Alcatraz Penitentiary. Abruptly the draft ceased and just as abruptly Nick doused his cigarette. Either the ghost of Hermann Goering walked von Stadee's ramparts in the early hours or someone had closed a door in the corridor. Nick inclined to the latter view but either way he was curious.

94

His hand found the hilt of the stiletto and in a moment he was slipping barefoot across the cold stone floor as quietly as any ghost. He heard stealthy footsteps in the main corridor and held his breath. Perhaps von Stadee had already checked into the background of Nicholas von Runstadt and found it wanting. If so the ball game might be going into its final innings now with the visitors trailing badly.

The footsteps moved purposefully toward Nick's door. He tensed, prepared for anything from a hand grenade or a cyanide spray to an old-fashioned burst of machine gun slugs. Then the iron-hinged door creaked and Nick felt a second draft. A form appeared against the moonlight and Nick stepped silently forward and wrapped one brawny arm around the intruder's neck, driving the point of the stiletto against the carotid artery with the other. Fragrant hair brushed his lips and a soft pliant body struggled silently against his grip.

"My God," Boots gasped, "don't you ever sleep?"

"That depends," Nick whispered. "What in hell are you doing up here?"

"I came to put a laurel wreath on the hero's brow. I hate to admit it but you looked pretty good in there today."

Nick scratched the back of his neck with the stiletto and contemplated the upturned face of the girl.

"What happens when the great man reaches out in the night and finds no Boots beside him? Or was it his idea that you come up here and bump me off quietly for beating his famous record?"

"Oh, shut up," the girl said. "You know why I came." In the half light she reached behind her and unzipped the back of the silk dress. When the dress rustled to the floor, she unsnapped her bra and drew her long slim legs out of her panties. In the cold moonlight, Nick could see her body slim and white and her eyes dark hollows like a witch's mask. Then naked, she stepped forward and pressed herself against him. Her slender arms encircled his great back and her mouth was hot and wet against his. Her writhing body wanted to devour his massiveness and her quick hands became roving things that caressed or attacked with a frantic off-beat rhythm. Under her passionate attack Nick felt his own excitement soaring. He picked her up in his arms to take her to the bed but she twisted free and pulled him down to the hard cold stones.

"Here," she gasped. "On the stone where it's hard and clean."

Her naked body was before him, young and vulnerable but with a lascivious knowledge of womanhood. Mercilessly she drove herself between the hard body of the man and the more impersonal hardness of the stone floor. When she lay stretched full length, spent and gasping, Nick picked her up, carried her to the bed and lay beside her. He could hear her sobbing quietly beside him.

"I adore the man," she whimpered, "he is so hard and beautiful. Why does he despise me?" She turned a tear-streaked face to Nick. "Tonight was the worst yet. He made me use a hot iron for over an hour and sat staring at the wall with this funny smile while his flesh was scalded and all the time I just wanted to comfort him and make love. God, I'm so unhappy."

Nick shook his head. Boots, who had some good qualities, loved von Stadee who in Nicks' book had none. There was no accounting for tastes. He let her talk and as she rambled on their intimacy and passion mounted once more. Later, somewhat consoled, Boots sat at the foot of the bed with her ankles crossed beneath her, smoking one of Nick's cigarettes and nipping on the flask of restorative brandy he kept in his luggage.

"I mean he says he has to take the Test of Excellence again to prove that he is worthy to be leader of the Teutonic Knights, which is foolish. I mean what in God's name has fighting got to do with it? Who else could be leader? You may be tough and all that but frankly you couldn't lead the Teutonic Knights across the street for a beer."

"Oh, I know I'm just a poor worthless creature," Nick grinned. "Not fit to carry the great man's bull-whip or whatever it is he fancies. But I know that if I were running the Teutonic Knights, I'd think of better things to do with it than kidnap obscure Swedish scientists."

"Are you kidding?" Boots giggled. Her giggling spilled the brandy on Nick's bare leg and down her own front. "This Swedish operation is just small beer, believe me. When Ricky is through he'll be running all of Europe and maybe America too. Let me tell you something, big fellow. Ricky is a doctor. I mean an MD and one of the best. With his brain he doesn't need to go around rumbling with Heinrich to show his stuff."

"I know it," Nick said.

"Well, I bet you didn't know that he was the guy who invented this bright blue death." Nick stiffened—a sensation as sharp as electric shock surged through him.

"Better ease off on the schnapps, kid," he said, forcing himself to sound casual. "I know your boy is bright but the guy can't make guys thousands of miles away turn blue and die overnight."

Boots giggled and Nick casually poured a generous slug of brandy into her cup.

"Oh, no?" she said. "Well, dig this. A couple of days ago Ricky came back from the lab and he was the funniest sight you've ever seen. It was the weirdest damn thing I've seen since King Kong fought the airplanes. I mean if you've heard of shocking pink you oughta have seen this. The future Chancellor of Germany blue from head to toe and flipped out of his skull . . ."

Nick's mind raced while the girl babbled on. Somehow he had to get the word back to Sweden that the indigo death rays were apparently non-existent. He'd need proof of course but that wasn't important. Astrid would be able to get started.

"He must have been pulling your leg," Nick said.

"Whasha mean, pulling my leg? Ricky isna' the kinda guy who goes in for jokes. You see all these guys are turning blue and dying an' they think it's something from outer space or something an' all it is is a thing Ricky dreamed up in the lab. . . . He shaid he'd finally perfected the strain so that no expert in the field could tell that it was an unknown virus or wha'ever it was."

The girl was nodding now, sprawled backwards across the bed. Gently Nick removed the brandy from her hand.

"When does the Count go to the laboratory?" Nick asked. "I know a little about viruses myself. If he's got what I think he's got, I know a place where I can make a fortune for him with it." The line was crude but Nick had to keep her talking.

Boots' laughter was loose and uncontrolled. She caught Nick's hand and pressed it to her body while her head lolled backwards.

"He'sh got alla money he needs, lover. Besides, you come here to talk or make love, huh?" Boots' grin spread sloppily across her face. Unsteadily she tried to pull Nick toward her. "Allus passionate when I drink . . . never drink too mush . . ."

"The virus, Boots, the virus," Nick urged.

"I have a little bacteria that goes in and out with me . . ." Boots sang in a drunken monotone. "Cute little, bright little, blue little bac . . . ter . . . ia . . ."

A hollow laugh split the silence of the halls, a laugh that Nick had heard not so long ago in a shadowy amusement park in Denmark—a vicious insane laughter that Nick had vowed to quench once and for all. He sprang from the bed, stiletto in hand, and rushed toward the door but already the laughter was dwindling down the dark corridors of the castle.

"Thash Loki, the dwarf," Boots laughed idiotically from the bed. "He knowsh thish castle better than Ricky himself, sho don't bother chasin' after him 'cause you'll never, never find him. Come here, big fellow, and help me finish off the night."

Nick turned and looked at the girl. She lay with her legs spread invitingly and singing with drunken pathos under her breath.

"Oh, Loki's quick and clever, but Bootsie wants a man ..." Presently she drifted off into sleep. Shortly before dawn Nick woke her up and sent her clumsy and bleary eyed back to her room.

For some time afterward Nick stood at the casement and watched the light come up. It was a long way to Washington and, to face facts, there was a good likelihood that Nick might not live to bring the word back to Hawk in Washington. Yet, he would have no way of reaching Gustav the waiter until much later tonight. Just the suggestion of what was happening here in these remote Bavarian hills would enable Hawk to arm himself and prepare for von Stadee's takeover. And to secure or move America's Air Defense headquarters before the Chinese had a method to ruin it.

As if to reinforce the urgency of the situation, as the dawn broke the sound of trumpets was wafted across the silence of the early morning hills. Nick saw troops of well-armed combat teams supported by armor moving out across the valley starting their daily maneuvers. Maneuvers that would pay off when von Stadee decided to move against the West German government.

Could von Stadee do it alone? He would need help but not that much. Luther, Hitler, Castro, Marx and Mohammed ... the names of other men who had almost single-handedly changed the course of history for better or worse floated through Nick's mind.

He only hoped the crew-cut little waiter called Gustav was on duty tonight at the *Deutschland Über Alles Tavern.*

Dawn broke over the walled university town. The first workers appeared outside their doors, rubbing sleep from their eyes, and mounted their bicycles to pedal doggedly through the streets to another day's unrewarding labor. Those without bikes walked, oblivious to the charm of the ancient arches and alleys and bridges. Outside the door of an obscure café a figure stood motionless, unnoticed by the occasional worker and patient as the stones themselves.

Presently the door opened and Lang, the waiter, appeared. He bent to unsnap the lock of his bicycle, ignorant of the watcher a few feet away.

The animal eyes of the watcher were older than time and cold as Arctic seas. They glittered now as the time for action approached. The will was as steadfast as that of a hungry wolf but it was the creature's nature to be stealthy. He came forward in great bounding strides. The victim looked up, saw him coming, cried out and tried to run. The victim ran like a frightened mouse, without any thought as to where he was going. He sped toward the deserted street, hearing behind him an animal noise that was a cruel travesty of laughter. He gave one agonized scream for help that echoed futilely down the sleeping street and then a great hand fell on his shoulder and another caught him by the head.

As luck would have it, no early rising worker witnessed the sudden flurry of violence along the quiet street or saw the great hulking man catch the smaller one, who had run for his life, break his back with a single blow and then tear the head from the body with a hand that seemed more like a paw.

The head of the waiter Gustav Lang rolled unnoticed into a well-kept flower garden. The hulking killer threw the headless body over his shoulder and marched back toward the potting shed where the victim had kept his bicycle. There he stuffed the headless body inside the door and walked unhurriedly down the street. The street led to a larger street and that led to an even more populated thoroughfare. The hulking man plodded steadfastly forward oblivious to the workers beside him and to the blood on his face and hands.

Nick's arms were pinned behind his back by the strongest man he had ever encountered. He handled Nick like a baby and made old Heinrich look like the proverbial ninety-pound weakling.

Count Ulrich von Stadee regarded Nick with the faintest trace of a smile.

"It is nice to learn that you are not entirely invincible Herr von Runstadt. You may let him go now, Einar."

The iron arms that held Nick suddenly released him and gave him a shove that sent him sprawling to the floor in front of the Count.

"You might explain to me what you were doing in the lab area, Herr von Runstadt."

"I got lost," Nick said sullenly, getting to his feet. "I was trying to find the range director and the next thing I knew your ape jumped me."

Von Stadee laughed. "Einar is not an ape, or if he is, he is a very special sort of ape. He is a Viking and close to a thousand years old."

Nick turned and stared in astonishment at the man who had just captured him. The great hulk of a man stared back with the deep uncommunicative eyes of an animal. He looked old all right, but with the ruddy good health of an aged fisherman. Fifty-sixty years, maybe.

"Save the legendary Nazi-pagan stuff for your college recruiting campaigns," Nick said sourly. "I wasn't born yesterday."

The Count laughed and shook his head.

"The wisdom of common sense. It always manages to outsmart itself. Einar, let me assure you, is indeed a Viking. He was part of a crew found by a German polar expedition buried in Arctic ice shortly before the war. When my father sent me to Argentina in 1943 we managed under the greatest difficulty to bring five of Einar's crewmates and himself with us under refrigeration. Einar is our only success in resuscitation, the others suffered brain damage a thousand years ago or we lost them during our experiments to revive them. Naturally, I would like to share Einar with organized science. There is so much that full research teams could learn that is impossible by myself. Look at him. Am I not something like a god, Herr von Runstadt? After a certain amount of power and knowledge, don't you think a man changes in quality, becomes more than a man . . ." Von Stadee let the sentence trail off.

"Still I did not bring you here to talk about anthropology. For many good reasons I do not yet trust you enough to explain why I want that Swedish scientist, but I do. While you are probably an exceptional officer, Herr von Runstadt, the fact is that you are valuable to me only as a way of achieving Astrid Lundgren."

"Fine," Nick said cheerfully. "I'll go to Stockholm and get her for you. There will be a slight added charge but nothing exorbitant."

"On the contrary, my dear von Runstadt, you will go nowhere but about your duties here. You have told me that Fräulein Lundgren loves and believes in you. If this is true, a simple note in your handwriting will suffice for the plan I have in mind."

Nick nodded, masking his disappointment. The idea of a trip to Sweden with von Stadee paying the expenses had come like a breath of hope to Nick. Now he would still have to rely on Gus, the waiter.

"How do you hope to get anything out of her once she's here? The stuff she works on is so advanced that you could torture her for months and all she'd have to do is change a letter in a three-page equation and it would take you a year to find out if she were lying."

Von Stadee regarded Nick quizzically over his clasped palms.

"For your edification and in order, perhaps, to save me a great deal of trouble, Herr von Runstadt, I will demonstrate."

He pressed a button on a control board in front of him. A segment of the paneled wall slid back and revealed a bank of television receivers. A picture tube lit up to reveal a scene that reminded Nick of a scene in a seventeenth-century insane asylum, Bedlam or Charenton perhaps. Wretched, emaciated creatures sat dully around an entirely empty room. Not one moved.

"Catatonic schizophrenics, Herr von Runstadt? No. Observe."

The Count spoke briefly into a telephone and presently two burly white-coated attendants walked into the picture and affixed electrodes to the skull of one of the inmates.

Suddenly all the motionless haggard creatures were in action, tearing at the keepers, their hollow dark eyes alive with a strange frenzy. Some crawled on their knees; others, women, offered revolting loins to the pleasure of the men in the white coats. One of the keepers moved his mouth, saying one word, and suddenly the ragged horde fell backward, cringing, whining and trying to climb up the bare walls in their obvious panic. Nick's brow furrowed. Von Stadee chuckled.

"You have seen the most dramatic part. Like electricity you can only see the effects, not the thing itself. What we have here are my guinea pigs in experiments which have hitherto been conducted only on animals. Perhaps you are aware, my dear von Runstadt, that certain centers of the brain, to put it simply, control the pleasure and pain functions of the body. By stimulating these electrically, you can provide your subject with pain beyond the agony of the martyrs or pleasure beyond anything imaginable to the mind of man. A pleasure that makes indefinitely prolonged sexual intercourse seem trivial, a pleasure as unimaginable to one who has never had it as the joys of heaven."

The Count's voice dropped slightly and he chuckled.

"Unfortunately this pleasure has its drawbacks. Since it is perhaps a million times stronger than the pleasure of any known stimulant such as morphine, LSD, et cetera, it is also a million or more times more habit forming. Three seconds of it can make a man a vegetable. That's how I control Einar, by the way, by alternating the pleasure and pain. Since he is valuable to me, I have never sent him on a 'trip' of more than one second's duration."

"Who are those people?" Nick asked quietly. The Count grinned.

"They are what the Americans would call 'foulups.' Men and women who have entered our order and then betrayed it deliberately or through error."

"And that's how you're going to get the anti-laser formulae out of Dr. Lundgren?"

"Of course," the Count said.

"And what if you blow it right out of her head?" Nick asked.

"My surgical abilities are not your concern," the Count laughed, "at least as long as you stay in line and refrain from 'fouling up.' For your information, however, loss of memory is impossible. This brain control is without a doubt the strongest motivation known to man. After a certain point, she will be only too glad to remember."

The Count looked at his watch.

"You will excuse me now, please. Be good enough to transcribe this note to Miss Lundgren and bring it to me in the morning. I am very busy right now. It seems a café waiter, a certain Gustav Lang, was murdered in the town today and I must assure the authorities that it had nothing to do with us."

Count von Stadee rose.

"*Auf wiedersehen,* Herr von Runstadt. Pleasant dreams."

CHAPTER 10

NICK LEFT the Count's study and headed for the stables. Gustav Lang the reporter was dead. There was no way of getting a message out of the Count's castle and after tomorrow Nick's cover as a neo-Nazi sympathizer would be blown. As if it weren't half blown already with that dwarf Loki spying on him from around every corner. But Astrid would get the note in Sweden and Larson would refuse to let her come to Germany and von Stadee would know he had bought a pig in a poke. Nick would have no warning. He would just turn up dead like Gus Lang.

The stable smelled of the sweet tang of hay, horse urine and manure in almost equal proportions. Nick picked out a big bay mare that looked as if she wanted a little work and drew a saddle from the tack room.

"New, aincha?" said the wizened old churl who guarded the tack.

"That's right."

"Well, yer better keep to the paths once yer off the main grounds. Go wanderin' off into the woods and you'll get a bum full of cyanide and ruin an expensive horse."

Nick went very Prussian.

"When I need advice from a stablehand, I'll ask for it," he said, mounting. The mare was restive and wanted to run but Nick held her in check as he moved out of the stable yard and took her at a walk along the woodside. In the gathering dusk he would be hard to spot from the castle.

For everything under the sun there is a time, a time to war and a time to refrain from war. Right now it was time to get out while the getting was good. Nick owed his life to his ability to make big decisions fast; he hadn't gone back to his room. Packing even what he could take in his pockets would have been insane. Instead he had chosen surprise. Even while he was in the Count's study he knew that when he walked out the door he was going right on out. All the way to Sweden or into the arms of the Count's killers.

Nick left the main grounds of the castle and urged the mare up the steep bridle path that led into the woods. Already in the dark, in the shadow of the trees, the mare tended to shy at the noise of birds whirring through the pines. Nick stroked her silky shoulder and attempted to soothe the nervous animal.

"Whoa, easy girl," he said. "I hate to think what I'm going to have to do to a magnificent animal like you but there's no help, darling. Just the same, girl, let's not worry about it until the time comes, okay?"

The horse nickered and shied at a passing rabbit. Nick laughed.

"Should have remembered that you weren't an English-speaking horse." He switched to German and rambled gently on to the animal while his mind raced. At the top of the rise he stopped and took a long look at the castle and its buildings as if to engrave their positions in his mind. He had used his time in the lab well before old Einar caught up with him. And although Nick didn't know a spore from a virus himself, a good scientist would. And there was a big hell of a difference between delivering one scientist signed and sealed into von Stadee's mercy and sneaking one in to get the true word on the famous blue virus which apparently amounted to so much war paint. Nick could never prove to the international scientific community that the "indigo rays" were a clever contrivance to frighten scientists away from working on the laser defense, but Astrid could.

Where he judged the main road came closest to the fenced-in forest, Nick reined the mare off the trail into the woods. Even in daylight the cyanide traps would have been difficult to see. At the last light of day it was purely a matter of luck whether Nick made it or not.

The horse itself gave Nick unwilling help. She shied and started around easy areas of open ground and took him through bushes. Sometimes she stopped altogether and Nick had to kick her ribs soundly to get her started but he never forced her to go forward. Whenever the horse stopped dead he walked it wide around the spot that made her nervous. It was maddening, slow work made especially frustrating by the knowledge that his unscheduled departure might already have been found out and that even now patrols might be setting out after him through the woods or waiting on the roads.

Then ahead of him he saw the high chain link fence that protected the Count's acres from the gaze of the curious. Was it electrified? Nick doubted it. The white signs at twenty-five-foot intervals along its length said: *Achtung . . . Verboten . . . Trespassers will be shot.* Nick had perhaps fifty yards to go. Suddenly a hare started up under the feet of his mare. The mare bucked and screamed and took off straight ahead through the bush, her ears flat against her head and her eyes rolling. Nick couldn't have held her in if he were Willie Shoemaker. He watched the fence getting closer. Thirty yards, twenty yards and then he heard the snap of the spring gun go off. He got his feet out of the stirrups and flattened himself against the horse's back.

The mare took the pellets with a shriek of pain and went down hard but now Nick was in a good position to bail out without breaking his neck. In a moment he was on his feet and staggering away from the wildly flailing feet of the agonized horse. For a moment he contemplated using the Luger to put her out of her misery but the sound of the gun shot might reveal his position. The cyanide would do the job quickly enough.

Finally he turned and picked his way delicately to the fence. By the time he reached it, the horse lay quiet and the only sound in the woods was the late flying birds among the pines. Nick began to climb the fence. There was barbed wire at the top but it bent toward the road to keep people out. Nick threw his tunic over it and climbed down the other side without any difficulty.

Then he began to walk along the darkening road. In his billfold were about twenty dollars in Deutschemarks and he had a long way to go. When a car came by he concealed himself in the underbrush. When he heard the heavy noise of a truck motor he would hitchhike. It was sixty kilometers to the university town and the Count would have noticed his disappearance long before Nick could walk the distance.

It was a far cry, he thought as he ambled along, from the movie version of the life of a government agent. Presently a manure van appeared which took him halfway to town. After that he picked up a ride with a couple of farmers who passed a bottle of cognac back and forth while damning the government. Nick joined in heartily, adding a couple of indictments that they hadn't thought of. In an hour the lights of the university town appeared down the road and then the farmers announced that they were going to stop for supper.

"You come with us. Then ve take you on to Frankfurt."

Nick shook his head. They were parked in front of the town's main restaurant, the *Deutschland Über Alles*, which Nick knew would be crammed with members of the Teutonic Knights. Nick was too well known because of his victory over Heinrich to pass unrecognized.

"Stomach's a little queasy and I'm tired as hell," Nick said. "If you don't mind I'll just catch a little sleep in the cab."

Both of the big farmers slapped Nick on the back, at the same time nearly driving him through the cab window.

"A little schnapps fix you up in no time, ja. You come with us. Ve eat together."

Nick was stubborn. Finally the farmers strode off toward the lights of the café laughing loudly together. Nick slumped down in his seat and kept his hand near the butt of the pistol. The Knights were out in force, looking for the man who had so brutally murdered the waiter at the café.

Nick waited an hour for his friends to come back while mobs of German youths flowed by the cab of the truck, red-faced with beer and the excitement of the chase.

"Stop all strangers. Question everyone," they cried back and forth. The interrogation amounted chiefly to cornering coeds and stout-bosomed farm girls and demanding their names, addresses and telephone numbers, but among the cadres of youths Nick noted a few harder-eyed, more mature types from the castle with revolvers on their hips. Von Stadee hadn't been caught napping too long.

Nick eyed them all stonily from the cab and chain smoked. Another hour passed and still the two farmers failed to appear. He was contemplating hot wiring the truck and seeing how far he could make it when the two men in coveralls came unsteadily out of the café.

When they saw Nick still in the cab they stood hawhawing on the street and shouting with surprise.

"Ach, our queasy friend is still with us. What do you make of that, Herman?"

"I can make nothing at all of it, Karl. I think it ish a problem for the professors up at the university and not for poor farmers who smell of pig dung no matter how hard they wash."

Nick would gladly have silenced the two humorists with the Luger but reasoned the shot might draw some attention here in the center of town.

"Then I guesh we must take him to Frankfurt, Herman."

"Ach, thash a fact, Karl."

The two men climbed ponderously into the cab of the truck and after several false starts succeeded in arriving at the main road to Frankfurt.

"Von Stadee hash all hish men out looking for a murderer instead of sheeking the traitors who shold us out to the Russians and the Americans. Not like ol' von Shtadee at all."

"Ach, goot man von Shtadee," nodded Karl. "Knowsh how to treat bloody God damned Americans, ja."

Flares appeared in the road and lanterns waved. With a great deal of cursing, Herman slowed the truck to a stop. Several young men with carbines stood uneasily in the road and a tall blond officer of university age approached the truck.

"We have orders to check all trucks on the Frankfurt road tonight," the officer said crisply. He put a foot on the running board of the truck and waited. Herman stuck his big red face out of the truck and breathed in the blond's face for close to a minute before deigning to answer.

"An' jush where the hell were you *kinder*, when we were checking Russian tanks on the road to Stalingrad, huh?"

"Thash the spirit," Nick said grinning loosely and taking a long pull from the almost dead cognac bottle. "Jush where the hell were you when we were flying two dozen sorties a week against the B-17s, huh?"

"We shouldn' be mean to these darlin' children," Herman decided ponderously. "They mean well, but they don't know any better."

"I am a captain in the Teutonic Knights," the young man snapped. "And I mean to . . ."

"Lesh us three beat the hell out o' this captain and all his men jush to show him what it was like," Nick suggested jubilantly.

"Thash a damn good idea," growled Herman, "speshly ash they don't have no lousy authority to stop a lousy taxpayer. Ven ve fight ve fight together."

He opened the door of the cab belligerently. The captain shoved it closed again and turned his back.

"Three drunken farmers bound for Frankfurt," he snapped. "Mark them down and let them through. We do not save Germany by arguing with drunken pig farmers."

"Ach, victory," said Herman.

"And not a shot was fired," said Karl.

"Glorious," said Nick. "Have another cognac."

"You first," said Karl. "Ven we drink, ve drink together."

The truck grumbled once more into action and moved on past the sheepish-faced Teutonic Knights with Herman leaning out one side and Karl leaning out the other hurling obscene gutturals and Nick in the middle encouraging as he saw fit. After the checkpoint the night became a series of dark country roads and blaring headlights that flicked past leaving only darkness in their wake. Nick spelled the two farmers at the wheel and helped them back to the cab after the frequent cognac stops. Altogether, he couldn't have felt better. He had given von Stadee the slip and by dawn he was only a few kilometers out of Frankfurt. Hop a straight train through to Copenhagen with a bit of luck, he thought.

The sun was well up when the farmers decided to stop for breakfast. It was at a little stone inn set well back among the fir trees. They dragged him in above his protests that he had no money.

"Ve pay for breakfast. You goot man," said Herman who was no longer feeling loquacious. Stubbled and bleary eyed they sat down to breakfast.

Sometime later Nick looked up from his sausage to see a man with his head in an open newspaper. Nick's face filled one half of the front page. The headless brutally mangled body of Gustav Lang filled the other half. Nick didn't have to read the story to know that von Stadee had pinned the slaying on him.

Herman was deep in his coffee but Karl was gazing around the room in boredom. Just in the mood to read the back of another man's newspaper.

"Can you tell me where the Imperial Hotel is in Frankfurt?" Nick essayed desperately. "I have a friend but I have not been in Frankfurt since the war."

Herman looked up from his coffee, his eyes narrowed in thought, but Karl had already seen the picture.

"Look, Herman," Karl bellowed, "this is a murderer, the one they sought last night. He has made great stupid fools out of us."

Nick rose quickly. "Excuse me, fellows."

"It is the monster who decapitated the poor waiter," Karl was babbling. Both of the farmers hurled themselves at Nick at the same time. Nick measured the distance automatically. His right fist flickered out with the deceptive laziness of a heavyweight contender's and caught Karl on the point of the chin. The farmer went down like a man struck by lightning, but big Herman hurled himself on Nick's back screaming out for the police and assistance. It took Nick perhaps a second and a half to break Herman's hold and by that time he had roused the whole room.

"Look, everyone. It is the Beast of Bavaria out of the headlines. For God's sake, help."

Nick broke for the door with Herman and the rest of the room after him.

"Be careful, everyone," someone shouted quoting from the newspaper. "He is known to be armed and probably dangerous."

A great fat man in chef's whites appeared out of the kitchen and placed himself in the middle of the door. He was armed with a long-bladed knife for carving roasts. It was probably as dangerous a weapon as Nick had ever run up against and the fat man didn't look easily intimidated. You can't shoot your way out of this one, Carter, a voice within warned him. Hawk can smooth over dead spies but not civilians.

"Inform the police," the fat man said in a calm authoritative voice. "I shall detain him here while they come."

In the time it took to say this, Nick had scooped up a chair and with three heavy Germans hanging from his back, Nick drove for the door like a pro fullback going over for a first down.

The cook flourished the long knife at Nick and tried to dodge. The chair hit him legs first with all Nick's plunging weight behind it and the knife clattered to the floor. The cook exploded out the door with Nick and his captors behind him. For a moment there was a short melee in the driveway, but free of the knife's threat Nick made short work of the remaining men. He tried to be gentle with these good German burghers but he could only throttle his lightning instincts down so far. His hands and legs flashed in intricate dazzling patterns and the opposition went down panting and groaning and a moment later Nick was free.

He looked around. Behind the inn was a plowed field and beyond that were woods. They looked as promising as anything.else. Without wasting any more time, Nick began to run toward the rising West German sun.

CHAPTER 11

ALL DAY LONG the helicopters had been searching for him. They were still stuttering overhead at low levels above the trees. Every time Nick reached high ground he had looked down and seen men and dogs fanned out sweeping the fields. The Count had obviously seen to it that the murder of Gustav Lang received widespread publicity. Probably up there in his castle mimeographing press releases and thinking up newer and more hideous adjectives, Nick thought with grim humor. Humor was about all he had left now. The night was falling and he knew he needed sleep as badly as he ever had in his life. Only his supreme woodsmanship and the craftiness more usually found in hunting animals had kept him free this long. Even superb conditioning and rigid yoga training couldn't sustain him forever.

He had worked himself a little further north by brazenly hopping a freight train for a short distance. Then he lay in a swamp on his face for three hours while the search went on by him. He had taken a cab once at gun point with the fine carelessness of a man who was half out of his head. Because of that he had been forced to hide in an industrial coal bin for an hour. How far had he gone that day? Five miles? Ten? He hadn't the faintest idea. Now below him he sensed water, a lot of it. He staggered down the hill, seeing docks and river barges and loading warehouses.

Where there were warehouses, there were bums and for the time being that was the place too for Nick Carter. A place where a man could look as though he was wanted for murder and sleep in some rat's alley undisturbed.

The room was entirely white and the floor was gray stone. In the middle, stripped to the waist, stood Count von Stadee. His slim powerful back was marked with red lines like the tracings of a road map made of blood and the rest of his body glistened with sweat.

Boots Delaney let drop an instrument from her hand that any man who sailed before the mast a hundred years ago would have recognized instantly as a cat o'nine tails. The Count heard it hit the floor and rolled gingerly over on his back. He stared for some time at the trembling girl and then tossed her a shirt to put over her bare shoulders.

"I have won once more. All mistakes are washed away in blood. Ultimately it is all that men understand. After such as this I can face and dominate men before whom I would normally quake. Self-mastery is a fine thing." He chucked her contemptuously under the chin. "I was ready to be hurt but you could not do it finally. Thus I will always be your master."

"I don't think you understand, Ricky . . ." Boots began, but the Count did not let her finish. He picked up an agenda sheet and examined it for a moment. Then he dictated into a wall microphone.

"Von Runstadt is still at large. Top priority will be given among the Teutonic Knights and among all my enterprises, including the Von Stadee Drugs Ltd. and all companies and banks upon whose boards I sit, to the apprehension of the escaped murderer von Runstadt who is of the utmost danger to the Teutonic movement and carries enough information in his head to ruin us. All our political contacts are to be pressed into service in order to put pressure on the police authorities and, where possible, the military, to find this man at any cost. I am, of course, to be informed at once if he is apprehended. Unofficially and for our secret channels only I will pay five hundred thousand marks to the man who brings me his head." The Count chuckled briefly. "I do not need his body. As for the rest of the day's business tell Krupp yes, tell Volkswagen no and Lufthansa maybe. The rest can wait."

He switched off the wall mike and began to button on a tailored silk shirt and knot the tie. As he dressed he stared at Boots in the mirror.

"There is one last thing I forgot to mention, Boots. You will fly to Travenmunde where the elusive and resourceful von Runstadt will most likely try to cross the border into Scandinavia."

Boots stared silently, fascinated by the network of blood stains that showed through the silk of von Stadee's shirt.

"Did you hear me?"

"I hear," Boots said dully.

"Good. You will, as I say, fly to Travenmunde. All our considerable facilities will be at your disposal. If von Runstadt shows up somewhere else, you will instantly fly there. You, my dear, will bring me his head, no one else. It is only fitting since I understand that it was your loose tongue that originally gave away the secrets of our organization to the man."

"I—I can't," Boots said. The Count smirked and picked up the cat o' nine tails, handed it to her and turned his back.

"Strike," he snapped. There was a long silence, then the whip dropped to the floor a second time. The Count turned and looked at his watch.

"Max will have the Hawker Siddley ready in forty-five minutes exactly. You will be on it. You may use any method that your ingenious little wit may devise, but remember—the head."

The Count put on his jacket and went downstairs, whistling a Bach fugue.

The freight train was filled with coal. Somehow Nick seemed unable to escape coal recently. It had been a coal barge that had carried him down the river main and finally a coal train that was carrying him steadily toward the Danish border.

There was a clanking of wheels as the cars were

jounced up onto the ferry and switchmen bellowed directions. Then for a long time silence and finally Nick could feel the undulation of the boat at sea even through the heavy steel of the railroad cars. Furtively he peered out from under the tarpaulin and calculated his chances. How long had he been gone? Two days? Three days? Had the hunt died down? To hell with his chances, Nick decided. He hadn't eaten in thirty-six hours and upstairs was a damned fine restaurant. He dropped out of the freight car and made his way through the tightly parked cars in the empty hold to the stairs.

The grand salon was almost empty on this weekday afternoon. Nick walked over to a corner table and made a point of leaving his money out on the tablecloth where the waiter could see it.

The waiter filled his glass with ice water and left a menu, courteously ignoring Nick's appearance. Nick drank the ice water greedily. He had been on the run a short time but in that time it was easy to forget that anything good and simple like ice water existed. Already he felt better. When the meal was over he decided he would return to his freight car, catch a little sleep and wake up in Copenhagen. He wasn't wanted in Denmark so all he would have to do was avoid von Stadee's agents, which shouldn't be too difficult. That would be followed by a short flight to Stockholm and he'd be back in business.

Nick was drawn back to the present by a general rise in the noise level. The few passengers in the dining room were clustered at the windows chattering excitedly. Some were taking pictures. Nick looked up from his steak and saw only the gray sea mist that the afternoon sun hadn't yet burned off. He shrugged and went back to his steak. A moment later the ship's whistle blew, long abrupt blasts that indicated collision or other dire emergency.

Nick left his seat as shouting rose from the main deck area and the door to the deck flew open. Crewmen burst in on a dead run and Nick saw the cause of the excitement.

A dirigible hovered twenty feet above the deck of the ferry and armed men were dropping from winches onto the foredeck. And standing on the foredeck screaming orders with a machine gun in her hand was Boots Delaney. Her face was masked but Nick needed only to glance at the slim figure in black leather to know with whom he was dealing.

"Okay, Max," she yelled, "stand by."

More masked men burst into the dining room and raced toward him.

Nick promptly sat down and went back to work on his steak. The masked men ran right by him, through the long dining room and out the back door. As soon as they were gone Nick rose chuckling and started to walk quickly toward the men's room. The idea was to play for time.

He almost made it. Then the glass in the dining salon door shattered into a thousand shards as Boots' burp gun sprayed lead a dozen paces ahead of Nick's retreating form.

"Hold it right there, Nickie sweet, and get those everlovin' hands over your head fast."

Nick turned. Boots stood behind him, her slim black-clad legs spread wide to hold against the recoil of the heavy burp gun. A slow grin spread across Nick's stubbled face.

"Boots, baby, you're beautiful when you're angry." She didn't laugh.

"Let's go, *schnell*. Get the boys back fast," she yelled over her shoulder. "They've got thirty seconds after I'm back in the cabin to get aboard. Then they swim."

"We're all business today," Nick grinned.

"It's you or me, honey. Make up your mind. Are you going or staying?"

Nick decided he was going. As they came on deck, slings were waiting. Two men with guns covered him as he was winched into the cabin of the blimp. They shoved him into a corner and quickly frisked away his Luger and stiletto. Thirty seconds later the dirigible was rising away from the ferry. Wryly Nick noted a patrol boat speeding from Denmark toward the scene of the hijacking, five minutes too late.

As the boats beneath them dwindled to specks, Boots tossed the Tommy gun on the floor, stripped off her mask and stabbed a cigarette into her mouth. Nick winked at her. Boots grimaced.

"I'm supposed to behead you or something but that ain't my style. You're going back to Ricky and you can settle things between yourselves."

"What's the matter?" Nick chided. "No guts?"

"Don't bug me, man," Boots said tiredly.

"You won't get away with this," Nick said, trying to suppress the laughter in his voice.

"Are you kidding? The Teutonic Knights can do no wrong in Germany, especially when they catch a brutal murderer after the police have failed."

"You know Einar committed that murder."

"Talk to your lawyer, big fellow. I got other problems."

"Has your little Count been treating you badly, dear?" Nick asked sympathetically.

"Oh, shut up, will you? I've gotten in enough trouble talking with you already."

The conversation broke off abruptly. Four specks on the horizon were rapidly turning into deadly looking jet fighters. They came racing in tight formation around the balloon once, so close that Nick could make out the NATO markings on the wings and the group leader plainly signaling Max, the pilot, to take it down fast.

"Max," Boots yelled, "floorboard this goddamned balloon, will you? What in hell are you waiting for?"

"Das ish not ein eff von oh fife, Miss Delaney," the corpulant pilot bellowed. "Vat you tink, huh?"

The jets had gone upstairs in formation. Nick saw them high and far away. Then the leader turned on his belly like a shark striking at the surface and came barreling down on them. Nick watched closely for the pinpoints of light that would indicate machine gun fire. The crew scurried around buckling themselves into parachutes. Boots looked at Nick with disgust and then tossed him a parachute too. "Sometimes I think you've got a charmed life or something," she snapped.

Suddenly Max the pilot let out a whoop of joy. The lead jet had winged over at the last minute and zoomed away without firing a shot.

"Ve are ofer East Germany, Miss Delaney. Everytink coming up roses, now, ja?"

"Well you did it, sweet," Nick said. It was time to act before someone remembered to take away his parachute. His hand turned the switch on the deadly little gas bomb, Pierre, which nestled in his pocket. Its deadly gas was colorless and odorless and could kill everyone in the cabin within a minute, including Nick. His Yoga training had developed his self-control to the point where he could hold his breath for up to four minutes, but Nick had no intention of being around for four minutes more. Mentally he pinpointed his gun and his knife and checked the operation of the door.

And tried not to look at Boots Delaney. Good kid. Something of a criminal but put it down to bad company. Too bad. She had been ready enough to kill him earlier, though. Suddenly one of the crewmen pitched to the ground.

Boots looked at him and then sharply at the dying man. Nick could see her alert mind working and waited no longer. He bounded up out of his chair and snatched his Luger and knife from the man who held them. The German tried to resist but he was too weak now. Nick shoved him easily out of the way and hurled himself at the cabin door.

"What the hell!" Boots was on her feet reaching for a weapon but Nick paid no attention.

The dirigible wasn't making any great speed and the

door flew open instantly. A fraction of a second later Nick was falling through empty space with one hand securely grasping his rip cord ring.

The air was cold as it whistled by his ears and the earth flew frighteningly larger and closer each second, but still he refrained from pulling the cord that bound him to life. Instead he spread his body, using it as an airfoil to guide him as far to the West as possible, toward the border.

He had no altimeter on his wrist to tell him how fast his time was running out. A miscalculation would mean death. Still, if he landed in East Germany he was in just as much trouble as if he'd stayed in the dirigible.

Then Nick saw the barbed wire of the border fence running up the middle of a strip of plowed earth. White puffs of smoke appeared from the watch towers along the fence. Ground fire.

He could hear the crackling of the weapons and knew he was much too close. He gave the rip cord a violent yank, waiting with taut breath until the impact of the opening chute snapped him up hard in his harness. Then he was drifting down over the barbed wire. The guns continued to snap around him. Nick pulled the Luger out of his belt and opened fire. It wouldn't be very effective of course, side arm fire from a swaying parachute, but it relieved Nick's feelings no end to be striking back after days of running and hiding. And maybe just by luck he'd take one of the trigger-happy bastards with him.

The fence slid by sideways beneath his feet and Nick knew that he was coming down in West Germany. The wind blew him across the plowed earth. He landed in low bushes, rolled, slipped out of his harness and sprinted for the trees. The last of the bullets kicked up dirt around him and then he was safely in the woods.

One last look back showed the white nylon of a second parachute just billowing on the ground on the Eastern side of the border. Boots for sure. And high up in the sky a dirigible bobbed aimlessly with the shifting air currents, manned by a crew of dead men.

CHAPTER 12

STOCKHOLM. Finally. A clean, peaceful city built on islands, where the writ of the Diner's Club and American Express still ran and Nick was free to identify himself. He checked into the Hotel Bernadotte and waited at the desk while the clerk looked unsuccessfully for his name on the list of canceled numbers. A long hot shower later, Nick dialed Vice Admiral Larson's private line.

"Yes?" Larson said.

"Nick Carter," Nick said. "Hotel phone."

"Right," Larson said. "Any time at all."

"Good," Nick said. "Now."

Both men hung up at the same time. An hour later Nick ran his rented car into the mouth of the tunnel that led to Musko Island. Today, like every time he entered the great underground vaults of Musko, he was overcome by a feeling of uneasiness, an atavistic dread of an alien world. A little old to be getting claustrophobic, Carter, he chided himself. Once inside, the underground environment was easier to take. After all, there was nothing so strange about a tunnel. Or an underground parking lot. Or an elevator shaft or an office with the blinds down or unlit corridors. Most of the people in New York City might just as well live in Musko.

At the ground floor of the Security offices the receptionist told Nick he was expected and to take the private elevator right up to Vice Admiral Larson's suite.

On the way up he went over his story. It might be difficult to make Larson believe that he ought to risk Astrid Lundgren by sending her into von Stadee's lair to look for scientific proof that the indigo rays were nonexistent. But no one else had her reputation and, more

122

important, no one else was ready to believe Nick's story.

"Third office to the rear," the upstairs receptionist said. "He just got out of conference and said to send you right in."

Nick walked down the carpeted hallway, opened the polished wood door to Vice Admiral Larson's office and stepped back quickly.

The whiskered, cigar-chomping head of Security was dead on the carpet. His skin was bright blue and his eyes were open with the pupils rolled up under the lid leaving only the whites staring gruesomely at Nick.

For a moment Nick and the dead man faced each other silently, and then Nick exploded into action.

"Hey, Miss whoever-the-hell you are," he yelled to the receptionist. "Get some cops and a doctor up here pronto." He had forgotten where he was and had to repeat himself in Swedish. Then he ran through the room, the Luger cocked in his fist, kicking open doors and ripping down curtains. Nothing.

Already the corridor was filling up. Nick shouldered his way through swearing secret service types and white-coated medics to reach the receptionist's desk. She was weeping noisily to herself, her head bowed in her hands.

"Get me Dr. Astrid Lundgren," Nick snapped callously, "and hurry up about it."

Dumbly the receptionist obeyed, her eyes still streaming tears. Nick smoked and fidgeted while the call was put through. Vice Admiral Larson was as blue as all the technicians who had been working with the force field experiments but Nick was ready to bet that a really thorough autopsy would show that he had been poisoned or asphyxiated first. Then the hyper-fast multiplying spores had been added for color and effect. But in the current situation Nick couldn't prove it and no one was likely to believe that story except maybe Astrid.

"Her office says she's at home," the receptionist said finally.

"Well, call her there," Nick growled.

"I don't have her number here. I'll have to go to the files."

"I'll wait," Nick said with what he thought was exceptional charity.

The woman went off and came back and dialed Astrid's home number. She looked up, shrugging.

"All I get is a busy signal."

"All right," Nick snapped. "Keep trying. Tell her what happened and that I'm coming right over. Nick Carter. Tell her not to answer the door until I get there."

A thick, nauseating feeling of failure, so intense that his stomach churned, gagged Nick as he plunged down the elevator to his car. Larson's death had been hastily arranged. Certainly it would be traced sooner or later to von Stadee. There were some rules of espionage that neither side ever broke for their own good. That included bumping off the head of the other team. Agents, yes, Chiefs no. That meant von Stadee was first, desperate about Nick getting away and secondly, must be about to go for broke. No matter how popular the Teutonic Knights were in both Germanys they couldn't pull something like this without the other big powers insisting that they be disbanded. By force if necessary.

Therefore von Stadee must have felt that he was in a good enough position to tell NATO and the Russians and the French to go spit. Hmmmm ... rockets in Albania from China to von Stadee with love. The complications of the international situation whistled in Nick's head as he sped the rented car out of the tunnel toward Astrid's home.

Someone had sold out and Nick had a shrewd idea who it was. The car swerved wildly as Nick took the corner at full speed and raced down the causeway toward the Lundgren house. In ten minutes he saw it up on the bluff. He drew his breath sharply. Half of the house was a charred and twisted mass of rubble with smoke still streaming from the broken windows. Nick skidded the car to a stop and bounded up the long flight of stairs with the Luger at the ready. He kept on running right through the front door and raced into the living room searching for some sign of life.

"Astrid," he bellowed and listened.

Suddenly there she was, walking out of the kitchen with a drink in her hand, her lovely face pale and her clothes disheveled.

"Nick?" she said vaguely. "What are you doing here?"

"Hold on tight," Nick said, his words coming quick with the release of tension. "Vice Admiral Larson's been killed. I found him in his office."

The girl's drink hit the floor and she shrank back at if Nick had told her he'd come to kill *her*.

"Admiral Larson's been . . . Knute," she called out. "Knute. Admiral Larson has been murdered."

"Knute? Is he here?" Nick asked, a lot of things coming clear at once. "Where is he?"

Astrid was vague, trying to recollect herself.

"I think he's checking . . ."

"Right behind you, Carter."

Nick hurled himself to the carpet as a gun went off behind him. He kept rolling across the carpet until he came up behind a couch. Damn this Scandinavian modern stuff, he thought, worthless for stopping a slug.

"Knute!" Astrid screamed. "What's happening?"

Two more shots exploded in the wrecked living room and then Nick was returning the fire. The ex-ski star tumbled backwards into the next room and Nick had a chance to dive across the carpet and knock Astrid to the floor.

"You've got to be wrong, Nick," she gasped. "It was that dwarf, the one we heard laughing in Copenhagen. I heard that crazy laughter just before everything went up in smoke. Knute's here to help. He's too dumb to be a traitor."

"Knute's too dumb to know he was being set up for a double cross," Nick agreed. "But not too dumb to kill Larson and come here to kidnap you. He just didn't get the word they want you dead now."

The ski star's gun crashed again. Then they heard his footsteps as he ran out of the house. Nick stuck his head around the couch and looked carefully but all he saw was the calm sea out behind the wreckage of the house and wisps of smoke.

"Thank God he's gone," Astrid breathed. "This is becoming a nightmare. Something out of the worst nightmare you ever had as a child where those you loved turned into monsters."

"He isn't gone," Nick said. "He's got too much to lose if we live, but he gets out of the whole thing a hero if we die. Is there an entrance around back?"

The girl shook her head, then her green eyes came alive.

"Perhaps he could climb from one of the fir trees to the chimney and reach a window." Nick glanced up at the balcony that overlooked the conversation pit of the living room. He got up quickly and went to the other end of the room. Astrid stared at him as if he'd gone mad. Nick exploded out of a crouch, sprinted the length of the room, bounced up on a chair and without stopping soared up toward the balcony. His hands caught the floor of the balcony and he swung wildly in air for a minute, a perfect target, before hauling himself up and over.

Almost as soon as Nick was over a door opened. Nick flattened himself against the wall.

Knute appeared shoeless, walking so softly he would not wake a baby. A grin of triumph spread across his tanned face and his blue eyes sparkled as he lifted the pistol and peered down at the living room.

"All right, AXE agent, Carter," he said.

The smile was still brilliant when Nick put a bullet into

it and the back of the gorgeous blond head exploded into a raspberry mess against the wall. Nick watched the light turn dull in the blue eyes, then Knute sagged over the balcony and crashed down into the living room.

Astrid turned her face and leaned against Nick, gripping his shoulders the way a drowning man holds a life raft.

"Are you sure it was Knute, Nick? I can't understand . . ."

"Did you close that morgue door on me?" Nick asked impatiently. "I didn't think so. Neither did Vice Admiral Larson or Gustav Lang, the reporter. Brother Knute was the only other person who knew I was in there. It's a damn good thing Larson didn't let him in on our deal with von Stadee or we'd both be dead."

"What happens now?"

"Now," Nick said, "we get out of here. The neighbors must have called the cops and it's my turn to kidnap you."

"I don't have many neighbors," she said dispiritedly.

"That's good. But someone's going to be here soon so we'd better get a move on. I've got to get you hidden before someone establishes authority over you and says I can't do it. Among other things I've got to talk to Washington and tell them there's about to be a major war in Western Europe."

CHAPTER 13

NIGHT. The old DC-3 vibrated so badly talk was impossible. Nick stared out the window and let the flame from the exhaust manifold lull him into a semi-hypnotic relaxation. The only person to talk with was Astrid and she sat stiff and silent beside him, pretending sleep and probably wishing to hell that she'd never left her lab or cooperated with an American named Carter. Her bountiful curves were well concealed by the constricting suit she wore, the same casing of rubber that covers frogmen from neck to flippers in very cold waters. She was wearing six such suits, one over the other. So was Nick. He had thought up the idea as a defense against the cyanide pellets in the Count's traps.

Nick's estimation of Astrid, already high, had risen a couple of notches when he told her why she was making a night parachute drop in this strange harness into the woods of a man who wanted her dead. She had blanched visibly but said not a word. Now he couldn't blame her if she didn't feel talkative.

For Nick the night drop, if not routine, was familiar. The French had a phrase for it—the more it changes the more it's the same thing. The tension of waiting and wondering what would happen on the ground . . . the envy of the pilot who was returning to base . . . even the coordinates and the names on the map were the same— Mannheim, Stuttgart, Nürnberg, Munich. And he was going in again for much the same reasons he had gone in as a very young man.

His mind went back over his conversation with Hawk, the sparse old man who was the eyes and ears of America and sometimes, when absolutely necessary, the knife hand too. Nick had defended his highhandedness in kidnapping Astrid from Sweden by saying:

"Look at it this way, chief. I'd hate to infiltrate that lab alone and find out I swiped the ink bottle instead of the virus tubes. Also, I've got to prove he's behind the blue deaths."

There was a silence on the line while the old gambler balanced the risk against the reward.

"You have a point there, Carter. Do you really think von Stadee could take over Germany? CIA reports his membership at less than a hundred thousand all through Germany."

"He could take over Berlin with a quarter of that, if no one in the country raised a hand to stop him. And von Stadee has been selling the old military master race tomato juice in a new bottle pretty successfully. I don't think he'd run into serious opposition if he does it right.

"And if he does, he's the government which runs the army and has the power to conclude treaties. Like with China or anyone else."

"How's he going to bring off this coup?"

Nick shrugged. "My guess is he'll make sure, somehow, that the government in Bonn is severely embarrassed. With his connections there's a million ways he can do it. Then he stages a coup in Berlin and since the people will be angry at the present government and he appeals to the worst side of German politics, they'll support him. We take our bombs away. Unfriendly act, right? He goes to Mao and demands his missiles on the grounds that he's hampered defense against the laser so much that the Swedish and American hardened sites can be cracked open like a can of beer. Maybe he tells Chairman Mao a little white lie about how he killed the only scientist in the world who can defend against lasers. Maybe he even ships Mao a dead blond to prove it."

"Don't let your imagination run away with you, Carter," Hawk interposed, "but do go on. I'm finding this very interesting."

"All right," Nick said. "Even if the Chinese don't believe him, they'll give him the missiles just because they're a bunch of mean troublemakers who'd love to have a major power like Germany raising holy hell in Europe and friendly to them. He needs the Chinese missiles in order to take power but they need him, too. Now comes the nasty part. The other European countries are going to get awfully, awfully nervous once a militarist like von Stadee takes over. When they hear about those missiles they aren't going to wait for the bell. It'll make the shoot out at the O.K. Corral look like good clean fun."

"I suppose we could send a couple of divisions to Berlin," Hawk mused. Then he corrected himself. "No, I suppose nothing of the sort. Americans intervening in German affairs would bring a couple of hundred thousand 'friendlies' from East Germany across the Wall." He paused a moment.

"Well then, just what does our man on the spot propose to do about all this?"

"Go on in and get the evidence that von Stadee's been murdering citizens of other countries," Nick said promptly. "That way the West German Government can arrest him as a criminal before it's too late and while they still have authority. If we wait until he's running the show, it'll just look like propaganda."

Hawk hummed into the line.

"You may be right. We've been sitting on U-2 photos of the biggest damn missiles you ever saw being flat-carred to Albania and no one in Washington has been able to figure out what a little mite like Albania thought they were going to do with the heavyweight hardware. Now it makes sense. They're just being stored there waiting shipment to von Stadee's Germany. Just the same, remember if he gets hold of you, son, he can make a strong case for American interference anyway."

"Ah'm a slippery little varmint, chief," Nick grinned into the phone. "Easy to catch but hard to hold onto."

"Ah, the confidence of youth," Hawk sighed. "All

right, go ahead. But even if von Stadee fails, if you lose that girl we may end up way behind the Chinese in Air Defense. So don't start anything the United States Government can't finish," Hawk ended in a voice as dry as panhandle dust.

Nick did not laugh. Hawk might maintain his irony in the mouth of nuclear holocaust but Nick knew that the old man would sleep in the office until he heard from Nick again. The lightness of tone was based on a mutual trust and understanding built up over nerve-racking years working behind the scenes of momentous international confrontations.

The rasping of the intercom system broke into Nick's reverie and the laconic voice of the pilot said, "We're approaching the drop area, boys and girls. Five more minutes."

Nick roused himself and checked both of their outfits, taking special care with the transistorized walkie-talkies they would use to locate each other on the ground if they got separated. The plane was losing altitude fast now, moving in low over the pine forests of Bavaria. A very few minutes later Nick was out in the crisp night air descending fast. Waiting for him on the ground was the most dangerous man in Europe since the Germans were foolish enough to let a certain ex-corporal named Hitler walk out of a Munich beer hall alive.

He hung swaying in the vastness of the night waiting with drawn breath, then let it go in relief as a moment later he saw another canopy blossom beneath the indifferent stars.

On the afternoon of the following day, Nick sat in the shade of Bavarian pines surrounded by a complex of transistorized miniature radio receivers and tape recorders listening in shamelessly to the conversations in the castle. Bugging the castle hadn't really been difficult. The Count had elaborate anti-bugging equipment on all his lines but Nick had foreseen that and got around it by leaving some of the newest and most infinitesimal of radio transmitters at likely points around the castle. Because they weren't on any of the Count's equipment they couldn't be detected.

It was very pleasant sitting in the shade of a warm spring afternoon, smelling the clean country air, the tang of the pine trees and listening to the waterfall. Nick puffed on his cigarette and enjoyed his free time.

For a conspirator the Count had a very bad habit. His radiomen went on the air at a regularly scheduled time every day, which was one of the most amateurish blunders in espionage, but it made things much simpler for Nick, and he supposed even a superman couldn't think of everything. The sun warmed his forearms and he enjoyed the moment to its fullest.

The secret of long life. Down where the waterfall formed a pool Astrid was bathing and Nick was tempted to wander down and join her. He fought back the temptation. A minute later he caught some activity on his set and slapped the earphones over his head.

The Count's radioman was hard at work reaching fellow conspirators all over Germany. Nick's face was a study of concentration as he listened in on the lightning-fast German. He listened frowning for half an hour and then put aside the headset. He knew all that he needed to know. The rest, the other evidence that would convince a world court later, would be picked up on the slowly winding reel of micro tape but Nick had heard enough to know that he was going to have to go in tonight after the important evidence in the lab, or not at all. That was unfortunate. Nick would have preferred one more night to make sure that he had the trail through the cyanide traps perfectly cleared and his approaches to the lab foolproof.

His eyes were thoughtful as he watched Astrid walk up from the pool, a long towel wrapped around her robust curves and her white-blonde hair piled in a sodden mass on the top of her head. The towel left little to the imagination but what it hid was tantalizing. She came up to where he was sitting and stood over him, nearly naked and dripping.

"Miss Lundgren," Nick grinned, "did you know that you're beautiful when you take your glasses off?"

Her laughter was as clear and fresh as the mountain stream.

"I am so glad you think so, Mr. Carter." She sat down beside him and put one of his cigarettes between her full lips and lit it. The towel loosened as she bent, revealing smooth breasts and vulnerable gorgeous nipples. Go run around the castle a couple of times, Carter, he told himself, or take a couple of dozen laps in the pool.

To keep his mind on business he said, "It's going to be tonight, I'm afraid. Von Stadee is about ready to move. They're going to frame the American Government with some scandal and assassinate the Chancellor three days from now. There will be a carefully calculated rumor that the Army and Air Force are rebelling and von Stadee will seize power to 'restore order.' We've got to get the evidence that he's been murdering people tonight and get it to Washington."

Her laugh was just the faintest bit uneasy.

"That's what we came for, not an Alpine vacation on the Swedish government. It is a lovely day to die," she said, looking around at the clear sky and the towering pines. "I mean, if one has to die, what a lovely memory."

The towel fell a little lower and parted slightly where the full thighs, smooth as mother of pearl, joined her soft belly. Her green eyes were direct and challenging.

"If you weren't such a nice girl," Nick said thoughtfully, "I'd swear you were trying to seduce me."

She smiled and leaned over, kissing him on the mouth.

"How observant of you, Agent Carter." She let the towel fall entirely open. The statuesque body, white and full and firm yet without an extra ounce of fat on it, took Nick's breath away. She smiled and lay back on the pine cones, one perfectly sculpted knee flexed and her body spread to receive him. "I admit that I misjudged you, took you for another brainless golden boy," she laughed. "Naturally, I just discovered this on the afternoon I'm probably going to die."

"You aren't going to die," Nick said. Her long arm reached out and pulled him down to her.

"Show me why not," she murmured. Her hands slid under his shirt, treasured the molded iron curves of his chest, slipped the buttons open quickly and roved lower over the gridiron of his lower belly. As he slipped out of his clothes she reached behind her head and let her long wet hair cascade over her shoulders. Then her ripe mouth was exploring the ridges of his body and her long limbs twined themselves with his. Slowly at first the sleek cool body beneath him began to undulate.

"Now," she said softly, "we have a lot of wasted time to make up for and it will not be dark for a time yet. I want you to make love to me in such a way, Nick, that I will have something to remember during my last moments if things do not go so well tonight."

"I have told you everything will go beautifully tonight," Nick said lightly. But despite the conviction in his voice, the knowledge that everything might not go so well and that either or both of them might be killed, or worse yet, captured by the Count, was uppermost in his mind. It added a piquancy to their lovemaking, an earnestness and tenderness that only the knowledge that this golden afternoon might be their last could bring. She cried out softly, something between a sob and a sigh, and the hard resolute lines of Nick's face softened. He smiled as he looked down at the closed eyes of the beautiful girl who was making him the gift of herself. He was very aware of the clearness of the air, the sweet tang of pine and the heat of the sun on his back. If all soldiers were given an afternoon such as this before the surge of combat, Nick thought, for sure, wars would never cease. For there was a glory to sex before danger. It was for Nick the best vintage of the wine of life, tasted by a very few whom the gods loved well.

"Now, Nick now," she moaned through clenched teeth, "don't ever stop, I feel everything . . . never so much. . . . Please Nick . . ." The words trailed away to incoherence.

Under the mountain pines the two superb bodies fused for the final excursion into the jealously guarded territory of the gods where the pleasurable pain of their climax was as stupendous as the pain of birth and as sharp as death. They crossed over into another country, a rare kingdom that existed only when they were together in love and whose boundaries might never be fully explored.

But none of this was said. In the end, Nick lay back and cradled the full body of the girl in his arms and caressed her face which was still flushed with the exertions of passion. Words are superfluous where everything is understood. They lay together in silence savoring the clear beauty of the mountains in the late afternoon and talked little and when they did speak it was about trivialities. The afternoon was long and as the shadows lengthened it turned cold, but they lay together under an old army blanket, reluctant to separate and face the night. And again and again they made love for there was much to be said through the language of their bodies and a very short time in which to say it.

Eventually it grew dark and a crescent moon appeared above the pines. They dressed wordlessly. In the dark she watched big eyed as Nick armed himself and carefully checked his weapons.

"Haven't I read . . . Don't you carry a suicide pill or something?" she asked quietly.

"Some people do," Nick said. Then he grinned. "I don't believe in suicide. Do you?"

She laughed and snuggled up against him.

"Not if you don't, darling."

The micro tapes that contained the supporting evidence against von Stadee were long since buried. Nick gave her a last lingering kiss, then very deliberately erased the memory of the afternoon from his mind. Together they started down the Valley of the Shadow.

CHAPTER 14

TEN MINUTES past midnight by the radium dial of Nick's watch. The castle and grounds slumbered in the weak moonlight like an illustration out of Dali. What in hell was the girl doing in that lab, Nick fumed. She should have been back half an hour ago. He fought down the impulse to go in and look for her. Changing the signals on a line of scrimmage was all right for a professional quarterback but in espionage it could be fatal.

Fifteen more minutes passed. Then his keen ears picked up silent footfalls in the dew-drenched grass. He flashed his infrared light and grinned. Astrid was moving along the shadows of the Count's lab building with the savoir faire of a hardened cat burglar. A minute later she stood beside him in the concealment of the outdoor generator.

"Get it?"

She nodded, beaming as if she'd just won a National Merit Scholarship.

"I'm not really top notch as a bacteriologist, she whispered, "but I'm pretty sure this stuff is so much blue dye and definitely used on the bodies of our murdered scientists. As an added bonus I took a long look at a copy of the Chinese laser plans. They're nowhere near as strong as I thought they were. I'll have a working defense in two months."

"*Wunderbar*," Nick whispered. "You're a gentleman and a scholar and I hearby nominate you for several dozen Nobel Prizes. Meanwhile let's get the hell out of here. Someone may discover one of those dogs we stunned."

Before they moved, however, Nick took one of the two small sample cases she carried. The act was a grim reminder of the fact that they weren't out of von Stadee's

Germany yet and that the evidence of the Count's guilt was more important than either of their lives. Once he had the case strapped to his belt, they started swiftly away from the lab. Nick felt no misapprehension that his infiltration had gone so smoothly. As they followed the prearranged escape route, Nick reflected, not for the first time, that he would have been an immense success if he had chosen a life of crime. He wouldn't have done badly as a Fagin either, considering the speed with which Astrid was picking up the techniques.

A tap on his shoulder froze him in his tracks. His eyes roved the shadows until he saw the great arched back of one of von Stadee's hounds. His finger tightened on the trigger of the pellet gun that would put the beast instantly to sleep for an hour and a half which was better than killing the animals and leaving evidence of their visit. This time the gun was not necessary. Unsuspicious, the hound loped away from them across the rolling lawn and Nick and Astrid continued their smooth unhurried walk.

Plenty of time and perhaps two miles of easy trail to the place where Nick had broken out on horseback. Only this time there were two light, easily assembled motorcycles hidden in the woods and he had long since cleared a path through the cyanide traps.

Suddenly Nick drew up short. At the same time he felt two sharp taps which meant *man*! He pressed the button of his infrared light and let it play around the grounds. Behind him, he heard Astrid's involuntary hiss of fear as the infrared illuminated the stern, inhuman face of Einar, the man von Stadee had boasted of bringing back to life after a thousand years of something that was neither life nor death.

The Viking stood stock still staring directly at them as if the infrared were a visible light that gave their position away. Astrid's hand clutched Nick's arm and her teeth began to chatter violently.

"My God, what's that?" she gasped. Nick put his finger to her lips. There was no telling how keen the old Viking's senses were. Nick was ready to bet that they were as good as one of the dog's with the advantage of a brain that was at least semi-human even after von Stadee had finished fooling around with it.

There was a long fearful moment as they stared at the Viking. In the infrared light his harsh ugly features gave off a spectral glow. Then he took a slow step forward. And another.

Nick tensed like a cat while his mind raced. If he shot Einar the noise would bring the castle down on them and make escape hopeless. Quickly he made his decision.

"He's got us spotted. There's no point in both of us getting caught. I'm going to draw him off. You know the escape route. Use it."

Astrid's face was white in the moonlight and very serious.

"No, Nick. I will not let you be caught."

The controlled fury on Nick's face caused her to step back with fear.

"This isn't lawn croquet, lady," he snarled softly. "You'll damn well follow orders and get out now. Start moving out the minute I draw the Viking off and don't stop until you're across the border." His face relaxed into its familiar grin. "See you in Stockholm, beautiful," he said. Then he ran lightly out of the shadows into the moonlight and called out softly to the gigantic shadow that came deliberately closer.

"Einar, old boy. Over here."

He circled the Viking on dancing feet until he was leading him directly away from the girl. The Viking broke into a run and Nick quickened his pace. Nothing slow about old Einar. Nick was going to have to extend himself. They were both running hard across the lawn now but Nick's hard edge of physical conditioning was showing results. The Viking was losing ground at every step. His hand dropped to the belt of his tunic and came up with a short, broad-bladed throwing axe.

Waving the axe above his head, old Einar did something that Nick had not foreseen, didn't even know he could do. He threw back his head and uttered a strange and terrible yell, his old Norse battle cry. Perhaps the act of swinging his war axe and a man fleeing before him had touched some dead nerve of memory. Nick had never before heard so much as a grunt from the old Viking, but it was too late now for second guessing.

Abruptly Nick checked his finger on the trigger of his machine gun while the weird cry that had caused panic on the beaches of Northern Europe a hundred years before the Conquest echoed across the hills. Lights were going on in the castle and every dog on the estate was howling with fear. Nick decided not to give his position away by cutting down the old zombie. Let it come as a surprise to the Teutonic Knights that he had a machine gun.

With a fresh burst of speed Nick drew away from the old man and melted into the shadows just as the lawn became a pandemonium of baying animals, shouting men and stabbing searchlights.

The confused baying of the dogs gave way to a different note, the steady yelping of a pack working on a trail. By some mischievous twist of fate, they had picked up Astrid's trail instead of his own. From far away he could hear hoarse guttural voices, shouting orders. Whatever she did, Nick hoped to heaven that Astrid didn't lose her head and blunder off the escape route into the cyanide traps. He needn't have worried. There was worse luck in store for him that night.

A jeep with a heavy searchlight mounted on its rear whizzed across the lawn. By the light of the searchlight beam Nick saw a dispiriting sight. The dogs were clustered about a cowering Astrid and two men in boots were driving them off with rifle butts.

Nick cursed softly in the dark. His direction was clear. They had Astrid but they didn't yet know about him. Only Einar had seen him and Einar couldn't talk, Nick was sure of that. Under the circumstances, there was a damn good chance that a professional like Nick could get out and across the border in safety, and that was the procedure the way it read in the training manual.

Nick cursed again and threw the training manual away. The situation had changed, anyway. Before tonight Astrid had been an agent with necessary technical qualifications. But since she had seen those Chinese blueprints in the lab she was the one person in the West who had an appreciation of what the Chicoms were trying to do against atomic military sites. She was too important to be sacrificed.

Impotently, Nick watched as the patrol returned toward the castle with Astrid. He didn't fear the men. With his machine gun and grenades and the element of surprise, he could cut the patrol to pieces. But the sort of banzai attack he contemplated was ruled out by the likelihood of killing Astrid along with her captors.

Silent as any night marauding predator he slid through the shadows, contemptuously avoiding the patrols that quartered the grounds. When a dog growled nearby he dropped it with a tranquilizer, and once he heard a patrol leader talk knowingly about the woman leaving doped meat about the grounds.

Time was short. The confusion of the men in the castle must be capitalized upon before they got organized. Fortunately, he knew from his electronic eavesdropping that most of the officers who were quartered in the castle itself were in Berlin preparing for von Stadee's coup against the government.

But the great man was still in residence and as soon as he got a look at Astrid, he'd know that Nick was somewhere nearby and goodbye to the element of surprise.

It took Nick fifteen more minutes to reach the main gate.

The battle situation, he saw, was bad and good. Two guards with submachine guns stood in the light of the sentry boxes on the castle side of the dry moat. Okay. It would be touch and go as he ran across that bridge but he'd beat them. Behind them stood a jeep and on the jeep were mounted twin fifties with men to feed and fire them.

Nick didn't care much for that arrangement, but there wasn't much to be done about it. Either he was going in after the blonde or he wasn't.

As a great man once said, Carter, he told himself, here goes nothing.

Nick burst out of his concealment and sprinted over the crown of the bridge that arched the moat. The faces of the two guards were caricatures of dull-witted men trying to think fast as an obvious madman bore down on them out of the dark. At the same time, the light dawned on both of them and they raised the wicked-looking muzzles of their Tommy guns. Nick fired two sharp bursts from his hip and both guards tumbled backward and slammed to the cobblestones.

The noise of Nick's gun alerted the men in the jeep. One man sprang to the twin fifties and squeezed off a burst as Nick threw his length on the cobblestones.

The tracer bullets flared over his head and bounced still sparkling off the stone walls. Then Nick had his own gun in play adding to the racket in the courtyard. A moment later he yanked the pin of a concussion grenade and hurled it toward the jeep, just as the machine gunner started to depress the barrels of his weapons. The grenade went off in midair blasting all the men off the jeep and scattering them around the cobblestones like so many rag dolls.

The profound silence after the grenade exploded was somehow more menacing than the roar of guns. The corporal's guard on the jeep seemed small opposition for such an important stronghold.

Shrugging off his doubts, Nick got to his feet and sprinted for the door of the dungeon. He was pretty sure he knew just where he'd find von Stadee and Astrid.

The vast baronial hall where the officers of the Teutonic Knights customarily sat brooding over history and drinking to the glory that was Germany was now empty. Or almost empty. At one end of a long table sat Count von

Stadee with his legs in exquisitely polished riding boots crossed on the table in front of him. At the opposite end of the enormous table sat the dwarf Loki, his misshapen little form almost invisible below the edge of the table.

Astrid, unconscious and naked to the waist, lay on the middle of the table and from her head and heart wires ran to a small control panel next to the Count's hand.

The Count raised his head as he heard Nick's footsteps but did not otherwise move. Nick placed his back against the stone wall and covered the room with his machine gun.

The dwarf giggled.

"Put down your weapon, AXE agent," von Stadee said. "I have won."

"The hell you have," Nick growled.

The Count poured himself a fresh glass of champagne and sipped slowly.

"But of course I have won, Herr Carter. In a moment, if you do not throw down your weapon, I will activate either the pleasure center or the pain center of Miss Lundgren's brain. Which would you prefer to observe? Pleasure beyond mortal experience or pain beyond damnation?"

The Count chuckled loosely. Nick realized with a start of surprise that the man was more than a little drunk.

"In a moment I may activate your brain all over the wall," Nick said pleasantly, but inside himself he felt a cold knot of despair settling in his guts. As if reading his mind, the Count's lips curled.

"Come, come, Herr Carter. We both know that in the end the United States fears China's nuclear capabilities more than a resurgence of German militarism. You will kill no one as long as Miss Lundgren is alive."

The Count said something in a Scandinavian sounding language and the vast figure of Einar bulked out of the shadows. He wrenched the gun out of Nick's grasp with a strength that almost broke Nick's wrist and plucked the grenades from his belt like apples.

The dwarf laughed and clapped his hands.

"Ach, you approve, Loki. We have defanged the serpent," the Count said thickly, "and you applaud our triumph."

The dwarf bounded out of his seat and turned a series of handsprings up and down the hall. The Count watched him with glazed eyes and a vacant smile on his face. The smile faded as the dwarf, tiring of the acrobatics, strutted over to Astrid and sprang on the table. The obscene little figure bent and fondled the full body with both hands.

Nick swore aloud and started forward. The Count wagged a finger at Nick and grinned lewdly.

"All the martial virtues and gallantry too. Ah, what a splendid Teutonic Knight you would have made, Herr Carter, were it not for your decadence."

The dwarf was leaning toward Astrid again when Nick caught him by the scruff of the neck and flung him halfway to the wall. Count von Stadee laughed as the dwarf screamed in a shrill, feminine voice.

"That will be enough, Herr Carter. Another step and I will destroy that magnificent brain. In three seconds I can turn her into a blank-eyed moron who cringes or fawns at the lift of an eyebrow."

"What's to stop me? You plan to kill us anyway," Nick said. His fingers played with the activator of Pierre, the deadly little gas bomb. The trouble was that Pierre did not distinguish between friend and foe and Astrid would breath his deadly incense too.

The Count put his feet on the floor and rose unsteadily.

"It grows late," he said swaying slightly. "Duty calls. When I return, I will decide what is to be done with you two. In the meanwhile the good Einar will stand watch. *Auf wiedersehen,* for now. Come, Loki."

Nick accepted the lie. The Count walked to a door at the end of the room followed by the dwarf and turned with his hand on the knob.

"Perhaps it occurs to you to wonder why I am alone in

the night of my greatest triumph. In three days I shall be the master of Germany as I am sure you have guessed. Then Europe and who knows? America is not out of the question. But I am alone in this triumph because you corrupted Miss Delaney. I owe you a debt and in ten minutes it will be marked paid.

"The castle is about to explode. It will be very clear that the explosion was the work of American saboteurs attempting to destroy the Teutonic Knights and this will reinforce other plans of mine which I regrettably do not have time to tell you about. Be assured that I shall ride into power on the strongest wave of anti-American sentiment since 1941."

The Count began to open the door, then turned once more.

"You will of course attempt to escape. Einar will see to it that you don't. I wish you luck, Herr Carter. Once more *auf wiedersehen.*"

The room was suddenly plunged into blackness, and Nick heard the heavy door close and metal clank firmly into place. He ran quickly to the table and stripped the electrodes from Astrid's head.

How long had von Stadee said? Ten minutes? That door would take some breaking down. Nick remembered the place where Einar had dropped the grenades and began to grope in the dark. Then he felt a presence beside him and heard heavy breathing. A great paw shot out in the darkness and caught his wrist in a grip that was as impossible to break as reinforced steel. Good God, the Viking must see in the dark like a cat.

With his free hand Nick drove a karate chop to the Viking's face that should have split his skull like kindling. The grip didn't weaken at all but a sound of pain somewhere between an animal's growl and human speech bubbled up out of the darkness. Desperately Nick groped for his stiletto.

From outside came the snarling gargle of a helicopter rotor shattering the night's silence to smithereens. The noise increased in intensity and then dwindled as the chopper rose away from the castle.

Anytime now, Nick thought. Maybe von Stadee can control the explosion from the helicopter. The castle was about to be blown to hell under him but Nick was helplessly locked in his silent death struggle.

He summoned all his strength and drove his knee into the Viking's crotch. The blow should have killed but the only reaction from the Viking was an increase in the inhuman growling.

As he struggled, Nick's eyes became adjusted to the dark. By the dim light that filtered through the casement windows high above the floor he could see Einar's face, inches away from his own, blank eyed and pitiless. Nick strained until a red haze covered his vision, and managed to move the giant a couple of inches back, just far enough to free one hand to reach the stiletto.

Nothing had ever felt so good as the heft of the weapon in his hand. Now if he could free his arm to strike just once . . .

With an agility Nick wouldn't have believed the Viking possessed, his throwing axe was out and once more he raised the ancient war cry until the hall seemed to be some nightmarish echo chamber. The gesture left one of Nick's hands free. As he switched the stiletto he realized he was too late. That great axe which the giant handled like a toy would come driving down through his skull at the same time as his blade found the Viking's throat.

The eyes of the two men met as they drove each other irrevocably to their doom, and then a strange thing happened. It was too late to check their blows—they were committed—but the Viking's arm crashed down empty on Nick's skull as the stiletto plunged into Einar's throat up to the hilt. The axe bounced noisily to the floor. The Viking's blow, even empty handed, was hard enough to send Nick reeling to the far edge of consciousness. As Nick recovered he saw the giant sinking slowly. They were both drenched with blood.

Einar's grim visage broke for a moment into what might have been the beginning of a triumphant smile, and then he fell into the shadows and Nick was never sure of what he had seen.

That strange smile. . . . Einar had probably never met the man who could stand up to him since von Stadee had revived him. His warrior's instinct had flared briefly and then lost to the desires of a proud man who must be released from his servile bondage to von Stadee, a victim of dog-like devotion made possible through electronic impulses. Einar had in effect committed suicide rather than live as a slave. He sure took his God damned time making up his mind, Nick thought sourly. He wasted no time in further reflection.

One grenade did for the door. With Astrid on his shoulder Nick raced down the corridors into the courtyard. Luckily, the jeep's motor turned over on the first try.

Nick and Astrid were ten miles away when the residents of the valley were awakened by what they thought at first to be one of the worst spring thunderstorms remembered in that part of Bavaria.

CHAPTER 15

IT WAS COLD for a spring night. Fifteen below zero with the wind out of the northeast at more than twenty knots. Two men sat in the cabin of the great four-tracked Sno-Cat, mushing carefully along through the carbon-black night.

In the warm cabin, Nick's parka was thrown open, his uncut hair and stubble-lined face bent in concentration over the compass. He had to be very cautious. The snow, packed so hard that it was nearly ice, held deep crevasses that yawned beneath the Sno-Cat's tracks, waiting to drop them a hundred or more feet to a painful and certain death.

Somewhere to the east, Count von Stadee had prepared his last refuge by the water of the frigid Greenland Sea. In summer it was even negotiable by boats. Supplies and technicians could be brought in and politics sent out and the Teutonic Knight movement could live in a sort of suspended animation like old Einar the Viking or a deadly bacteria that can restore itself to life when the climate is more advantageous.

Killmaster steered the Sno-Cat through the great desolation, one spore moving after another, with a high, keening song of murder singing in his heart and a cool detachment is his brain about how he was going to do the job. Behind him Joe Shu leaned against a carton of blasting gelatin and spooned concentrated field rations into his oval, high-cheekboned face.

"Listen, Nick," the Eskimo said, "it is important that the machine guns come last and then into play very quickly. The temperature will rise with the sun but not much. We'll keep the guns inside until the last minute and

148

later we'll keep them firing to keep them hot. Otherwise, we stand more of a chance with seal knives, understand?"

Nick nodded. If Joe Shu said something was important, Nick had learned, it was. The great central icecap of Greenland was largely unexplored and to Nick it was an alien land where his life depended on the wisdom of the man in the cabin with him. There had been no time for the usual briefings and classes. Nick had been lucky to be prepared as he was for the trek, for it had been only three days since he first heard the Greenland lair mentioned by the Count's radioman.

"I think we're coming down toward the sea," Nick said. "We ought to be."

Joe Shu shrugged.

"Perhaps. I have been only twice this far north and then only as a very young man. We shall see, huh, Nick?"

The tractor swayed over the sparkling packed snow, as Nick attempted to parallel the line of the great Rheinhart Glacier down to von Stadee's camp near its mouth at Cape Despair on the Greenland Sea.

Suddenly Joe Shu smiled and his obsidian-black eyes glittered.

"Tomorrow there will be a fog in the early morning, you shall see."

Nick stared out of the frosted window of the cabin at the hard clear sky and shook his head.

"If you say so, Joe. It looks clear as a bell to me."

"No," the Eskimo said firmly, "there will be fog. But the good part is that we shall approach the camp from the leeward."

Nick's heart leaped up. He had been a warrior too long to miss the implications of the last statement. In the morning they would approach the German's camp invisible and unheard. Half their problems were solved right there.

Steadily, the tractor forged across the great dark void, carrying the trackers closer to their quarry.

Morning. The fog had crept in silently just before dawn, out of the crispness of the night, exactly as Joe Shu had predicted and the two men had been able to run the Sno-Cat up into the concealment of the morain protecting the Count's camp at the foot of the glacier. Through the wisps of fog, now burning off slowly in the cold morning sun, Nick could see the Count's headquarters hacked into the base of the glacier's ice and reinforced here and there with timbers. To one side was a steel mat landing strip, outbuildings, barracks and generators. Nick intended that very shortly they would all blow up.

Beside him Joe Shu hunkered in his furs and drew on a cigarette.

"I dunno, Nick," the Eskimo said. "This is the biggest damn dynamite job I ever handled. Ice is tricky stuff. You blow up dynamite on the glacier, no telling what will happen."

Nick nodded abstractedly, not really listening. He didn't much care what happened after his attack started as long as von Stadee's radio equipment went dead, cutting his communication with Germany and making him unable to reach his co-conspirators. The Count obviously hadn't known that Nick picked up the secret of his Greenland hideaway or he would have personally seen Nick dead before he left the castle and never mind the anti-American propaganda evidence. But he must have suspected some outside interference or he wouldn't have prepared this expensive hideaway in a land that perhaps had never seen a white man since the dawn of time.

"About ready for the guns?" Joe Shu asked. "We don't want any of those birds escaping." Nick looked curiously at the dark-eyed Eskimo.

"What's all this to you, Joe? I thought this was just another job to tide you over until it was seal hunting time again."

"The hell with the seals, man," Joe Shu said. "I'm a Danish citizen and I remember the war. German gunboat killed my father. I'm ready with the guns when you are."

It was a hell of a long speech for Joe Shu. Nick nodded and checked his watch.

"A little more time, Joe."

On the airstrip a twin engine airplane coughed into life. Nick could hear its engines running rough as the pilot tried to warm them up. Presently a party of men in parkas came out of the door of the main building and trudged across the hard-packed snow toward the waiting aircraft. Nick picked up his binoculars and swung them on the party. Beside him Joe Shu released the safety on his light machine gun.

"Now, Nick?"

"Let's wait until these Eskimos get out of the way. We don't want to cut down Danish citizens even if they do do business with a louse."

Joe Shu spat. "Them ain't no Eskimos, pal."

Comprehension came swiftly to Nick. Chinese. Whatever von Stadee was up to with a party of Chinese on the day he was supposed to be taking over Germany, it boded no good for America and the NATO countries.

"Aim well, Joseph, and fire at will," Nick breathed.

A second later, the still of the Arctic morning was cracked by the fierce, insistent chatter of the machine gun. The party on its way to the aircraft broke in confusion as their members started to fall. Half of them raced for the airplane and half of them sprinted for the protection of the headquarters building carved into the glacier. As Joe's machine gun picked up the group running for the plane and cut them down unerringly, Joe carried on a running commentary out of the corner of his mouth.

"Get the God damned travelers first and come back for the stay at homes. Hah, no damn Chinese in my Greenland. No damn Krautheads, either. Hah, take that, stay down you mangy walrus."

The machine gun continued to buck and chatter in his hands and the brass shell casings leaped and hissed in the snow. Nick's eyes were pinned to the barracks. Christ, what had happened to the time fuses? Maybe they should

have waited to hear those charges go off. Maybe the cold
had screwed up the timing mechanisms. Maybe, maybe,
maybe. Half a squad had fallen out in the packed snow
and Joe cut them down as they came out the door. Suddenly the building seemed to shrug once, then it exploded
into a million fragments. A moment later the crash of
noise reached Nick's position.

"That takes care of the reinforcements," Nick said
quickly. "Let's go."

Already the wiry Eskimo was slipping the flame thrower over his back.

"That's what I like about Americans," he grinned, "so
well equipped." Side by side the two men raced across the
snow toward the main door of von Stadee's ice palace
while the other charges they had set shook the earth with
the power of their explosions.

Sporadic rifle fire greeted them at the door. Nick fired
two thermite grenades on the dead run and threw himself
down to shield himself from the blast of hot white light.
By the time Nick and Joe came crashing through the door
there was nothing but corpses left to dispute their passage.

They were in a large hall lined with synthetic paneling,
and from the dead way their voices sounded, Nick knew
the room was constructed with trapped air between the ice
of the glacier and the room, which meant that it could be
heated and von Stadee could stay there winter or summer.
Behind the insulated room, however, there were long corridors of green ice leading into the interior of the glacier.

From far down one of these ice corridors, Nick heard a
familiar sound, the maniacal laughter of the dwarf
Loki.

"Let's go, Joe," Nick snapped. "Just keep sweeping
that flame thrower ahead of us."

Suddenly there was a rumbling louder and more sus-
tained than anything the explosive charges could possibly

have caused. An expression of concern appeared on Joe Shu's round face.

"Ice, Nick. Pretty soon the whole damn glacier will fall into the sea. You never can tell."

The room looked perfectly still but Nick could feel the movement in his stomach as if he were riding a boat in a heavy swell. He made a fast decision.

"Go ahead, Joe. Go back to the Sno-Cat. I'll join you but first I have to see von Stadee dead."

"You don't get combat pay if you don't fight," Joe grinned. "I'll stay with you and charge the American Government. Eskimo boy makes good."

"All right," was all Nick said. "Let's make it quick."

It was Musko all over again. The labyrinthian tunnels, the feeling of existing in a science fiction world. And always there was the dwarf's laughter leading them on, tantalizing them around corners of blue-green ice, leading them into hails of bullets. Pressing them and making them hurry more than they should. There was a sickening feeling in the pits of their stomachs as the glacier slid slowly into the sea.

Occasionally they ran into resistance. If the defenders fled, Nick let them go. If they offered resistance, Nick and Joe attacked with the flame thrower and the diehard Teutonic Knights became flaming corpses that slid down the melting ice and quickly became cold.

In some nameless turning they found the man who was to rule Europe holed up in a small cavern which they almost overlooked. Joe's flame thrower turned the Count's two aides into human torches and suddenly the man who had called himself "very like a god" was screaming for quarter from behind a pile of packing cases marked "frozen fish!" Nick held his fire while the Count crawled out with his hands high in the air.

"*Kamerad,*" he bellowed, "I surrender."

"Hold it right there while I frisk you," Nick snapped.

The Count did not very much resemble a great world

leader. His stubble was bright with frost and his burning eyes were glossed over with the sickness of defeat.

Suddenly the dwarf laughed again nearby. Somewhere overhead.

"Carter," the Count implored, his words coming thickly, "do you realize what you're doing? Give me twelve more hours and I'll make you rich beyond anything you ever dreamed of. Carter, for the love of God, *please*. We are both soldiers. . . ."

Nick almost had a moment of pity. This is the way a thousand-year Reich ended, he remembered thinking later. Behind the jackboots and physical conditioning there is a softness of the soul that is shameful to think about.

The dwarf laughed again. Nick spun on his heel and spotted the twisted little man on a ledge twenty feet above them.

The dwarf giggled and dropped a hand grenade down on the ice where it bounced once. Nick crossed the room and kicked the iron pineapple away and threw himself down on the floor as it went skittering down the icy corridor. He felt rather than saw Joe Shu's flame thrower and heard the ice ledge break away from the wall and the dwarf screaming. Then the grenade went off and the world became a maelstrom of noise and flying ice crystals.

In the confusion, he felt the Count's hands around his throat, squeezing with the grip of a madman. Nick managed to break the hold and regain his feet while the Count struggled vainly to hold him down. Nick drove his forehead into von Stadee's face and felt blood running down his own face.

"Fight, Count," Nick taunted, "fight for your destiny. Show me how you can be a fighting wolf."

The Count lunged at him. Nick ducked, caught the Count and threw him across the room to smash into the icy wall of the cavern. The Count slumped to the floor and stared at him with lackluster eyes.

Nick's grin was cruel as he pointed down the ice tunnel to the main hall.

"There's the road to Berlin, Count von Stadee. Why do you just sit there? It's yours for the taking."

The Count fumbled in his parka and came out with a long-bladed, stag-handled hunting knife. Nick looked him steadily in the eye. Reluctantly von Stadee got to his feet.

The bright blade of Nick's stiletto appeared in his hand. Then the Count, pale faced and red eyed, sprang.

There was a brief flurry, as blurred and fast as two fighting cats, and then a great jet of crimson blood gushed from the Count's throat and he crashed to the floor.

Nick stood over him a moment, then deliberately bent and wiped the blade of his stiletto clean on the Count's furs. By the time he got around to rolling him over, von Stadee's face had already frozen to the floor.

"Very good, Nick," Joe Shu said. "Excellent footwork."

Nick started. He had forgotten about Joe and the dwarf, Loki. He started again when he saw the headless body of Loki at Joe's feet. The evil head with the ugly little eyes rolled high up into the skull stared sightlessly at the ceiling some feet away from the tiny corpse.

Joe shrugged. "Eskimos are not barbarians. He fell on top of me and I miscalculated." His broad face broke into a grin. "American flame throwers very good but when the situation is truly serious, give me a seal knife every time."

"Damn," said Nick softly, "I had promised myself the pleasure." He stood staring down at the bodies of the dwarf and the superman, his face as blank and empty as the great Sphinx. Joe shook him by the sleeve of the parka.

"Do not worry about the manner of their deaths, Nick," Joe said. "Is it not written by the white man's God, that inasmuch as you do to the least of my brethren, thus I will do to thee."

Nick allowed himself the faintest of chuckles.

"I don't think that's exactly it but it might not be a bad rule. It wasn't what I was worried about, anyway. It just occurred to me that if I had been able to get von Stadee to name names I might have saved a lot of lives and trouble in Berlin tonight. You see the Count was risking nothing. If the coup failed he could stay holed up here."

Joe Shu raised his eyebrows.

"I wouldn't have said you had much damn choice," he said. "These are very interesting points and I don't mean to be chicken, Nick, but I think we would do well to get the hell out of here."

Once more Nick became aware of the fact that the cavern was rocking like a boat on an angry sea. Abruptly the two men in parkas turned and ran for their lives.

CHAPTER 16

THE NEWSPAPERS had part of the story and they wanted the rest. An old Washington legman buttonholed Nick at the bar of the Hotel Bernadotte.

"Haven't I seen you around, pal?"

"You must be thinking of someone else," Nick said politely while silently damning his luck. Unfortunately, the reporter had a good memory.

"Sure, sure, sure," he said to himself. "Carter's the name, Dick Carter. You're way up in the CIA or something."

Nick let the mistake ride. A grim silence was to be expected from CIA types anyway.

"Every once in awhile I hear something about you. Work with that guy Hawk don't you?"

Nick's smile was as innocent as a lamb at shearing.

"Purely on the technical side. I do a bit of work with ultra-sensitive film," he said, not untruthfully.

"Come on now," the reporter scoffed. "Some things are so big it's senseless to try to cover them up. All leaves canceled for American forces in Germany. Two B52 squadrons moved to Iceland and a whole battle group airlifted from Fort Ord, California, to England. Three German division commanders relieved of their duties overnight and the autobahns jammed with troops. All passage through Checkpoint Charley canceled until further notice . . ."

"Seems to me," said Nick, "that you ought to be in Berlin, not here."

"That's the funny thing," the reporter reflected. "All our tipsters say the answer's in Sweden, not Germany." The reporter shook his head slowly. "I dunno. After a while you sort of get a feeling for things in my business. You know what I feel now? I feel like it was Pearl Harbor all over again but this time the dive bombers were called back."

Nick shrugged. "I wouldn't know," he said. "I just got back from Greenland myself."

"Oh," said the reporter, losing interest.

Nick went up to his room. Swedish Government technicians were just leaving. Five minutes later Nick was in front of the newly installed picture telephone that was newfangled even for Sweden. At precisely the appointed hour, the screen lit up and Nick was facing the lean old man in Washington named Hawk.

"Did you finish the report?" Nick asked.

"Sat up all night reading it and couldn't put it down. I can't wait to see the movie. Just one point."

"Yes?" said Nick.

"It was pretty dangerous letting von Stadee escape to Greenland and then lone-wolfing it, wasn't it? If you had failed he could have directed his coup from there and flown in once the Teutonic Knights had taken Berlin. Then we'd have had a United Germany on the warpath with Chinese missiles pointed at the Champs-Elysées and Trafalgar Square. Pretty risky business, Nick."

"Well," Nick said reflectively, "we could have given the B52s the go code and had them level Cape Despair, but the coup against Berlin might have been underway by that time."

Hawk hmmmed for a moment, then looked up.

"On the brighter side, Nick, you might be interested to know that the FBI arrested an infiltration team of technologists similar to the ones you broke up in Musko. These were Chinese and they were sampling the rock strata around Cheyenne Mountain in Colorado where the NORAD headquarters are. The Chicoms, it seems, were getting pretty close with that laser of theirs, although I suppose they'll drop it now since it looks like we'll have a defense for it in next to no time."

They chatted further about technicalities for awhile and then Hawk signed off with his customary congratulations, notable for their brevity and lack of ego-inflating material.

For some time afterward Nick sat alone in his hotel room. A montage of faces passed before him. He saw an old university town with healthy, manly faces raised in song, dreaming of von Stadee's pleasant fictions of glory and duty because they were nicer and easier to understand than the perplexing and infinite subtleties of reality. Nick had been lucky, he decided. It was so seldom that you were able to point to an evil and do something about it. Usually evil led to evil with never a beginning or an end. *Histoire noire,* the French called it. Black history. He sat for some time with his scotch untasted before him.

Then came a knock at the door. Nick unlocked the door, keeping the Luger handy, but the nondescript character in the hallway seemed to be a bona fide delivery man.

"Package for Mr. Carter."

Nick looked him over, then took the box which was wrapped in brown paper and sloppily tied with string. Walking carefully to the couch, he set the package down and went to the bathroom and drew a tub. This well started, he returned to the living room and examined the package more closely. His name and address were written correctly in a sprawling girlish script. In the upper left hand corner someone had written:

"From the Secret Service of America, Urgent, Open at once and reply."

Nick grinned as he read the message. He was laughing out loud as he walked swiftly to the bathroom and gently lowered the package into the tub. When he could stop laughing, he raised his glass of scotch and said, "Thank you, Boots, wherever you are. You've given me my first good laugh in a month. God love the girl."

Still chuckling he drained his scotch with zest and

called the bomb squad. No sooner had he hung up than the phone rang again.

A sultry female voice which somehow managed also to contain a no-nonsense tone asked him if he were through with his damned endless meetings and reports.

"As a matter of fact," Nick said, "I began my leave exactly twenty minutes ago."

"I did too," Astrid said. "Began my leave I mean. They insisted that I take three weeks, can you imagine that?" Her voice contained a distinct note of outrage at a government which could encourage such criminal laxity. "I've never had that much free time since I was thirteen, darling. I don't know what I shall do with myself. I'm all alone. Even the workmen are leaving. They finished rebuilding my bedroom this morning, you know."

Nick laughed softly. "Hold on. I'll be right over."

Astrid giggled.

"I was just hoping you'd say that. So I told them to do the bedroom first and come back and rebuild the rest of the house in three weeks."

THE END